TO
TRAIN
YOUR
DAD

GARY PAULSEN

HOW TO TRAIN YOUR DAD

MACMILLAN
CHILDREN'S BOOKS

First published in the US 2021 by Farrar Straus Giroux Books for Young Readers
First published in the UK 2021 by Macmillan Children's Books
an imprint of Pan Macmillan
The Smithson, 6 Briset Street, London EC1M 5NR
EU representative: Macmillan Publishers Ireland Ltd, 1st Floor,
The Liffey Trust Centre, 117–126 Sheriff Street Upper
Dublin 1, D01 YC43
Associated companies throughout the world
www.panmacmillan.com

ISBN 978-1-5290-6930-3

1 3 5 7 9 8 6 4 2

A CIP catalogue record for this book is available from the British Library.

Printed and bound by CPI Group (UK) Ltd, Croydon CR0 4YY
Designed by Trisha Previte

MIX
Paper from
responsible sources
FSC® C116313

THIS BOOK IS DEDICATED WITH JOY
AND THANKS TO MY FRIENDS:

WES ADAMS

MORGAN RATH

KATIE QUINN

KRISTEN LUBY

MARY VAN AKIN

OLIVIA OLECK

SEAN FODERA

MELISSA WARTEN

LELIA MANDER

ANNE HEAUSLER

TRISHA PREVITE

KRISTIN DULANEY

JORDAN WINCH

KAITLIN LOSS

CATE AUGUSTIN

AND THE COUNTLESS OTHER FOLKS
AT FSG AND MACMILLAN WHO HAVE MADE
THIS RIDE SUCH A THRILL

DUMPSTER WISDOM

You need to know a little about me before you hear all the rest of the things I'm going to tell you about my life. Otherwise how will you know enough to understand what matters and where it all fits and how everything goes?

So.

My name is Carl Hemesvedt. Don't even try the last name. I'm not quite certain myself how it should be pronounced. My first name came from my mother, who passed away when I was six from some kind of disease mixed with a bunch of complications, which is how my dad puts it. She was wonderful, even if I only have foggy memories. My father says she was the best, but talking about her makes him remember she's gone and it hurts. So we hardly ever talk about her. Anyway, my mother called me Carley, which would be all right except it makes people think of a woman singer from before I was born, and I'm a boy who can't sing a hoot, so just call me Carl.

So I'm Carl and I can't sing and my age is just at the line between twelve and thirteen and I look like any other twelve-to-thirteen-year-old boy – here and there a pimple; hair that isn't cool; glasses so I don't squint; a body that seems to belong to some other person who doesn't like me very much.

In addition, I'm not good at sports (which I don't even try anymore); I'm average to poor at school (which I sometimes like, sometimes don't); I've got no brothers or sisters so it's just me trying to make sense of my father (more on that later); and finally, according to my dad and the reason for this book: I'm rich.

Only I'm not.

Not even close.

But that's not how my dad sees it.

So.

First week of my summer holidays, and we were sitting on the edge of a dumpster behind the supermarket that's in the shopping centre, sitting up on the edge looking down, smack in the middle of approximately a hundred and thirty-two thousand flies, just sitting there looking for stuff to salvage because my dad says supermarkets throw away a lot of perfectly good food, when he suddenly announced:

'You know, we have a rich life.'

Really, he said that.

As we were dumpster diving for food.

And if that's not crazy enough, here's how we live: We have a small trailer outside of town down along the river on five acres of dirt and mud, with four – you can come count them if you want – trees. Not big trees, no shade really, just four skinny trees next to a semi-scroungy trailer. There's electricity and a television, which my father never watches, and we can get internet connection, which my father never uses, but only by swiping the Wi-Fi signal from a nearby warehouse for a moving and storage company, and we have a shed that houses two pigs and eleven or twelve or fifteen or four chickens. The count varies from day to day because sometimes a few of the chickens – the smart ones – take it on themselves to leave. The not-so-smart chickens not only come back (I don't know why), but every now and then, they'll bring a new chicken with them. I don't have a clue where they get the new ones since we are surrounded by – in addition to the previously mentioned warehouse – a plastic shopping bag manufacturer, a ready-mix concrete supplier, a sheriff's impound lot, a school bus depot, an office furniture wholesaler, a shipping transfer station, and a garage for city rubbish trucks. There are no neighbours with chickens, or even houses with people, for that matter.

Add to the picture you're forming of where we live – our rich-life kind of place – a rebuilt, recycled, rehabbed 1951 Chevy half-ton pickup made up mostly of dents so deep you can see little puddles here and there in the bonnet after a rain (a truck, my father says, is not only immortal, but an absolute classic), parked in the mud near the trailer, and you get a rough idea of how rich we really are.

The truck has, I kid you not, an antique AM radio with what Dad says are vacuum tubes instead of transistors, so it doesn't come on right away but has to warm up first. It works, but only seems to get country songs and some crazy fast-talking man whose voice slam-booms loud enough to make your ears bleed as he offers to sell autographed pictures of biblical heroes including Jesus Christ.

Oh, there's a garden. A huge and extensive garden that we keep alive with the river water pumped by an old sump pump my father repaired – he's a true marvel at fixing things and making them last (for example: the old truck).

We grow all the vegetables we eat, although sometimes I swear they taste a little like the solvent and chemical run-off that we think are illegally dumped in the river by the nearby businesses. We feed the pigs leftover scraps from our own food, like potato peelings and cuttings from the garden, and stuff from the dumpster behind the supermarket, and every autumn a man comes with a small stock truck and takes away the pigs.

A week later he brings back pork chops and bacon and hams wrapped in white waxed paper with stamped labels. We put the packages in an old rejuvenated freezer (*see* 1951 Chevy truck, page 4, sump pump, page 5), and after we forget (a little) about the individual personality of the pigs (which is the reason we never name them in the first place), we have meat for a year.

My father says, whether you buy the meat in a shop or you raise the livestock yourself, you cause the same end for the pigs, and if you take responsibility for your own meat supply, then at least you know it's higher quality and you're not being quite as hypocritical. Same as a tomato you grow yourself. Or eggs from your own chickens. But the whole pig-growing-and-eating process bothers him all the same, and when the truck comes to get our animals, he has to turn away and not watch them leave.

Pooder, who is my best friend and who I see every day even when we don't have school, says he likes our place better than his (more on that later). His real name is Peter Haskell, but he insists on being called Pooder because there was an old-time actor named Peter Haskell who had a bunch of bit roles on TV shows he can't remember the name of, and he doesn't want people to confuse them.

Anyway, Pooder says we – my dad and I – are about three-quarters of an inch from becoming vegans or at least vegetarians because of how we raise our own meat and then feel bad about eating it. Considering that Pooder lives on hot dogs, Peperamis, and chicken nuggets (which he admits are a sludgy goop extruded – great word, *extruded*, it means pressure-squirting leftover chicken bits into nugget-shaped moulds – and then deep-fried in fat), and has never, literally never, eaten anything that didn't come in a box or a tin or a to-go carton, he thinks vegetarianism is something on the order of a crazy cult religion.

Pooder says if I ever become a full-on health-food fanatic, we'll still be best friends except that he won't want to walk too close to me or get sneezed on in case he might catch it.

I'm not offended by that, but I did start to keep a little distance from him in case the extruded-meat-loving thing might be contagious, too. Because I once saw him eat an entire large tin of those little grey Vienna sausages with his fingers, then drink the juice even though it says on the side of the tin they are made of something called – wait for it – meat by-products, which, my dad says, are lips and eyelids and noses and the skin around other body openings and maybe even roadkill because if you say something as vague as meat by-products, you're as good as admitting you know that it could be anything. Dad says that in these giant factories they go ahead and feed whatever's left over around the meat processing plant through a big old grinder and let it hit the extruder and boom, there's your meat by-products right there.

You never know, Dad says, you just never know what you're getting from so-called Big Meat.

I don't want to make anybody sick with talk of industrial-waste flavoured veggies and mystery meat, but I thought you should know about my dad and Pooder and how they think, because they figure into the story we're working on here.

So you've got me, Dad, Pooder, and the chickens, and then, of course, our dog, Carol, who is a rescued pit bull we found limping alongside the road near a part of town where you don't want to go unless you are looking for trouble.

Carol is all scars from where bad people had forced her into illegal dog fights, but she's very sweet to us and super protective about anything she thinks belongs to us, including people we're friendly with, but everything else is just plain in for it, and she's absolute murder to any skunk that comes wandering along the river and makes a run on our chickens. She tears them to shreds and scatters the strips around the garden, and since that happens at least once a week all summer long, she always smells so bad flies won't even land on her.

Dad loves her, but he also says she sits on our

little porch gazing over her world watching and waiting for anything that she perceives as a threat so she can go into attack mode. According to him, she's a loving, land-based white shark, and if you could hold her up just right and look into her mouth, you'd be able to see straight out her butt. He calls Carol a killing tube who also happens to like sitting on the sofa like a person, getting hugged, and watching television, before going to sleep next to you in bed on her back snoring like an old drunk.

What's not to love, he says.

By now you've probably got the idea that Dad's a really nice guy. And you'd be flat-out right.

He's friendly to everyone he meets and he's always been good to me, so I can see where it might become confusing to learn that the time came when his way of thinking started to drive me absolutely nuts and I couldn't stand it or him or the way we lived another minute.

TWO WAYS TO BE RICH

Because the thing is (and isn't there always a 'thing', sogotg that clearly has to change?), Dad has – what's the right word? – *philosophies*. Yes, that describes it; he has philosophies that he lives by that make perfect sense to him, but aren't always quite the way the rest of us look at things.

Like when he said we were rich.

He thinks money is just stored human energy. And why gather and store useless paper money – sometimes he even calls currency ertogs, which he claims was a type of money used by our ancestors in the Middle Ages – when you can use the energy itself and bypass money altogether?

This is strangely logical since we never seem to

have any money anyway. That doesn't affect Dad much, or at all, because he honestly believes we're actually rich. Not only not poor, which I would argue we clearly are, but doing better than great. He works odd jobs here and there, bartering.

That means he doesn't get paid for cleaning and restaining Mrs Petrakis's back deck, but that she sends him home with homemade baklava and three recyclable foil trays of moussaka because that's the kind of good stick-to-your-ribs food that freezes well.

And he doesn't get a cheque for patching the roof and hanging drywall on Mr Aitkins's garage ceiling to cover the hole where the rainwater dripped through the rafters and made mould, but he walked away with a full socket spanner set that Mr Aitkins's worthless son, who's not good with his hands and never calls to see if he can be helpful to his own father, didn't deserve to inherit anyway.

So when we were sitting on the edge of the dumpster the first week of summer holidays and my dad said that we were rich, I was caught off guard with the timing, but not, to be honest, by the substance of the conversation. He went on to say that it's a matter of something he calls timely historical perception, which means it's all in how you look at it compared to things in the past.

'We live better than European royalty used to live,' he told me as I sat next to him on the dumpster counting flies and looking for food to salvage to feed the pigs we were raising to eat later in the run-down single-wide trailer where we live. 'Way better than your average medieval king in a castle.'

'How do you figure that?'

Whether I asked or not, I knew my dad was revving up to share his thoughts on wealth and it's good manners to be an active listener.

'They didn't have electricity, which meant they didn't have refrigeration, which led to a lot of spoiled food. We don't have to deal with that problem.' He paused and I knew he was thinking of the freezer he'd tinkered with until it worked again. 'Plus, we have running water and a toilet to take away our waste so we don't get sick.'

'Ah,' I said, hoping we were nearly done with this conversation, which had sharply veered away from modern finances and toward archaic plumbing.

No such luck; Dad was on a roll.

'Don't you want to know how they pooped then?'

'Uh—'

'High up on the castle wall there was a hole with a little ledge where they sat and, you know . . . They called it the "Long Drop Convenience", because of gravity.' He nodded thoughtfully. 'A lot of what they dropped probably wound up floating in the moat, which was not the most hygienic way to handle things. But it definitely made their enemies hesitate before swimming across the moat to attack the castle if the drawbridge was raised.'

My father was always practical in the weirdest possible way. In the unlikely event we ever came into possession of our own castle and moat, I would never have to worry that he wouldn't know about its proper care and maintenance. His admiration for this ancient plumbing system made sense in light of his high regard for Carol and her skunk-killing; they're both nothing more or less than savvy home-protection strategies to my dad.

Pooder, as I thought he would, completely lost his mind when he heard about all the sanitary talk. He almost worshipped my father, thought he was a genius, and never passed up a chance to talk about bodily functions so, when I told him of the Long Drop, he nodded. 'He's talking about sewer trout.'

'I beg your pardon?'

'That's what sanitation workers call what we leave in the toilet.'

I cringed, already gagging a little from the residual odour on my shoes after having spent the afternoon in a supermarket dumpster, putting wilted lettuce and bruised bananas in a bucket for the pigs.

Pooder, however, was smiling, obviously proud of my dad's knowledge, and probably wondering why I wasn't embracing the opportunity to learn more about castle protection vis-à-vis human turds from an obvious expert who had clearly done his research.

Pooder's mind works a lot like my dad's; he loves going off on conversational tangents and he thinks my dad knows the most interesting facts that we never cover in school but still need to know.

But all this is aside from my real problem with my dad, which is the business of not being rich when he thinks – no, really believes – that we are.

Which had always been okay with me except . . .

There's a girl.

WE MOVE ALONG

Well, not just *a* girl. *The* girl . . .

Her name is Peggy and she has green eyes that make me think I'm looking into deep water, and thick red hair, and across her nose is the exact right amount of freckles placed in exactly the right order. She's in my year at school and everyone likes her and I have never ever ever seen her be catty or crabby or fake to anyone ever, which is something like a miracle in middle school, if you ask me. And I fell head over heels completely in love with her on the last day of school when I heard her laugh in the hallway. I must have heard her laugh a million times, as I've known her since kindergarten, but Pooder says when you know, you know – about soulmates that is. And I just knew.

Only, she doesn't know I exist. As a guy she might want to spend time with.

And I do want her to know I exist, as a guy she might want to spend time with, and therein lies the main problem I have with my dad.

I don't fit in.

Because of the way we live.

Even though we are richer than a medieval king, according to my dad, and don't have poop in our moat, our lack of ertogs, or dollars, or bitcoin, or what passes for wealth in the modern day, means I don't, can't, spend lots of cash on the right clothes or have any of the other kinds of things that would make me socially acceptable.

Or even noticeable.

Pooder says I'm not lookatable material. He also once said I was dotty. But he was going through that British phase of his where everything was 'dotty' or 'smashing' or 'cricket'.

His phases usually only last a week or so, except when he was convinced he was descended from Viking raiders and was swept over with his need to find a coast he could raid and pillage. He finally had to settle on a midnight attack on Ulf Peterson's garden where he was going to steal tomatoes and eat them like apples. Because he said that's the way a Viking would eat them, all tough and snorting with juice running down their chins into their beards, only he doesn't have a beard, and Ulf Peterson caught Pooder before he reached the tomato plants. Ulf Peterson was a fanatic gardener who had been having trouble with raccoons and was sitting outside in the dark to catch them; that night he caught a Viking raider instead and that's also when and how Pooder found that Viking raiders were not pain-proof when it came to hoe handles being wielded against Viking backsides by angry gardeners.

My father, of course, says it doesn't matter that I don't have clothes that make me fit in and help me be lookatable to Peg, that all that stuff is just for show and having it is like living on a movie set – all glitz and no quality. And what we're about – again, according to him – is quality.

Here's a good example of how my dad regards us and quality:

I decided that I wanted a good-looking, all-purpose bicycle. I had mastered two-wheelers when I was little and had even gone through a BMX phase, but I wanted a sleek twenty-one-speed touring machine that I could use for really going places. And, of course, for getting noticed and being more lookatable.

But they cost money.

Real money. Government-issued, legal tender recognized by and traded within a capitalist economy.

A new, relatively good, all-purpose, usable bicycle might go for several hundred dollars and, if you took a plunge in the deep end of the pool, could even run as high as two or three thousand bucks for a really sweet touring bike.

I didn't want to go that pricey – which I naturally understood we could never afford – but I did want a nice, sturdy bike to go on some adventures this summer and ride to school next autumn that would maybe help me take a stab at being accepted, or even just noticed, so I could at least try to fit in and talk to the other kids who hung around the bike racks before the first bell. And by 'kids', I meant Peggy. Because emerging from the school bus between a gaggle of geeks with their heads stuck in books and a bunch of hyped-up troublemakers was nowhere near as cool as the picture I had in my mind of pulling up to school on my new twenty-one-speed touring bike, casually leaning back in the saddle, riding no hands so I could give a cool nod and a jaunty wave to everyone milling around the front door. And by 'everyone', I meant, of course, Peggy.

But when I mentioned wanting a bike, my father set me down with a notebook, pencil in hand, and said: 'Let's jot down exactly what you are looking for.'

And even though I knew I was cooked, totally cooked, I said: 'I know we can't afford a very expensive—'

'Tell me what you want, or rather need, in a bicycle.' My dad is always reminding me to check myself: *'There's a difference between want and need, son. Make sure you always say what you mean there.'*

'Tell me what it is you think you need,' he repeated, 'and we'll work it out.'

Which is what I had feared going into the conversation and, as I predicted, exactly what he eventually did. We, that is he, 'worked' it out. With energy, not money.

Resigned to the inevitable, I wrote the list he wanted and handed it to him and then – knowing how flexible his timing can be and how pressing my need for a bicycle was – went on my way. I knew him well enough to be certain that he was never going to buy a bicycle for me and might even forget about the idea entirely. I turned my attention to figuring out how I could earn enough money at a job somewhere to self-fund a bicycle.

'You could sell a kidney,' Pooder suggested as we sat by the river trying to catch some catfish. 'Rich people with a lot of money and bad kidneys are always spending fortunes for them, and you've got two. Or a lung. You've got two of them as well. Big money in kidneys and lungs. You read about it all the time.'

'What in the name of the printed word have you been reading?'

'Mysteries. And I see stuff like that on television. I watched a movie where some crazy man was running around knocking people out and taking their kidneys to sell to rich people. Guy carried a cooler with ice in it to keep the kidneys from spoiling. Said buyers like them fresh.'

'I worry about you, Pooder. All the time.'

He snorted. 'I'm not saying we go around stealing them. Just find a buyer so you can sell one of yours. Get ten bicycles. I'm only trying to help out. I've even got a good little cooler we could use that I picked up at a garage sale.'

I studied him for a long time. He was smiling that little corner smile like he's only half kidding – but then he's almost always smiling – and it may have been that he was in a good mood because he'd just bought an amazing little drone, only slightly dented and missing the instructions, at another garage sale.

He said he saw it as an opportunity to set a new altitude record for a live frog.

'Thank you, Pooder, but I think I'll pass on selling a kidney.'

And all this time, while we were fishing and messing around with his drone, my dad had been off doing his dad thing – spending energy instead of money.

Out on the northern edge of town an old man named Oscar lives on a ramshackle piece of land that makes our place look developed and downright ritzy. I never heard a last name. People just call him Old Oscar. I'm not sure if anybody would spend enough time with him to get his last name anyway because he has apparently never discovered bathing. Or even washing. The smell he leaves when he walks by, followed, I imagine, by a greenish cloud filled with various insects, makes you think of old deserted pigpens and spoiled potato salad that's been left in the sun for a whole weekend or raw chicken you forgot about in the back of the fridge. And I say this as someone who sleeps with a pit bull who smells like skunk. But he has ten or so acres of dirt and brush, and to call it a junkyard, or even a dump, would be shooting well below the mark because he never, absolutely never, throws anything away, and when people discovered that Old Oscar 'kept' things, they started to bring the clutter they cleaned out from their basements or attics or garages to him.

Oscar always accepts whatever people want to leave, nods toward the rear yard, telling them to drop their stuff 'out back with the other junk that sort of looks the same as what you've got there'.

I am 100 per cent certain that every time Pooder mentions buying something at a garage sale, he means he found it in Oscar's yard. He only pretends not to love Oscar's heap of stuff because he knows how I feel about my dad being Oscar's number one customer (*see* old truck, page 4, sump pump, page 5, deep freezer, page 6).

'Oscar's got mountains of stuff that people don't want anymore,' Pooder said, reluctant to give up the kidney-for-sale suggestion so quickly and reminded of another source of kidneys as we watched my dad unload a box from the truck after visiting Oscar's place, 'so I have one of those feelings that if we dig deep enough in one of Oscar's piles, we might find a kidney the rich people didn't get to yet. Won't be any too fresh.'

Because Oscar is very old and has been doing this for his whole life, there are huge individual piles scattered around the ten or so acres – one of cooking pots and frying pans, another of stoves, ruined water heaters, a tower of old dishwashers, more than a few hideouts for stray cats (so you can pick yourself up a new pet at the same time you go looking for a spare part for your dishwasher that leaks), and near the end of the yard, an enormous tangled mess of discarded bicycles stacked up over thirty feet high.

So.

My father adores Old Oscar and his piles of junk. They fit in perfectly with my dad's philosophy of spending energy instead of money, and to illustrate how handy my father thought Oscar and his wealth of supplies (that's what he calls it, not a junkyard, not a dump, not a potentially hazardous hoarding situation, a 'wealth of supplies') could be, he virtually rebuilt the truck we owned – the 'classic' – from the ground up with what he sourced from Oscar's heaps. It is important to repeat at this time that, although the truck ran perfectly, didn't use much oil, and started on a dime, it looked – going now by Pooder – like only slightly warmed-up crap.

I'm not being mean; that's the right word.

Crap.

Because the only thing Oscar has more of than junk is rusted junk. And Dad is more impressed with function than form; he says it doesn't matter what it looks like as long as it works. That's important to remember for later. It's also important to keep in mind that form over function is what gets you lookatable if you are twelve going on thirteen.

On the back of our property, we have an old machine shed that my dad turned into a workshop e works on what he calls his 'projects'.

go in there alone and disappear for hours, creating and rebuilding things that he thinks will make our lives better.

He came out once with something like a double-powered super-blender that sounded like an F-16 jet fighter taking off because he wanted to make 'healthier' peanut butter from raw organically grown peanuts 'in only seconds'. The first time he used it, he forgot to hold the lid down and it blew loose and we spent hours trying to scrape the peanut butter off the ceiling (the stains are still there; Dad calls them an authentic kitchen aesthetic and won't paint over them). And Carol, who happened to be in the kitchen at the time, still doesn't enter that room without growling at the blender, and she won't even get close to a peanut butter and jam sandwich. This, I should point out, from the exact same dog that shreds and eats skunks, and, by the looks of her scars, came out the winner in more than a few fights (probably other dogs, Dad says, but could even be bears, maybe a honey badger or two; that part of town, anything is possible) and therefore fears nothing on earth.

Pooder thinks that my dad is not quite normal and more along the lines of a quirky mad scientist, but he 'honours the dedication and mission focus he applies to the execution of his goals'. (This was during Pooder's I-want-to-be-a-SEAL-team-member phase, which lasted until he tried to do a hundred and sixty-five push-ups after reading that's what SEAL-team members do just to warm up for a big day of land, sea, and air special ops, including but not limited to secret insertions and dangerous extractions of high-value enemy personnel and terrorists around the world. Pooder lay on the ground in a puddle of tears and spit moaning – only he called it a manly whimper – for nearly an hour after only sixteen attempts. After he was done dry-heaving, he decided that maybe being a Navy SEAL wasn't enough of an intellectual challenge for him and that maybe he'd do better as something like an electrical engineer or a professor of linguistics instead.)

Right after I gave Dad my list of what I wanted, no, *needed*, in a bicycle, Pooder and I started to do experiments with his relatively new drone – although the less said about that the better, except to say the frog probably achieved something close to terminal velocity when his little harness broke at three-hundred-eighty-nine-and-a-quarter feet (still 10.75 feet on the right side of the law, drone-altitude wise, that is, the government's rules about flying frogs being harder to pin down), and we later referred to this experiment, with downcast eyes and our hands over our hearts, as the 'gravitation-ally induced high-velocity frog measurement'.

We were pretty well occupied taking notes and making plans for more successful – and by that I mean less lethal to amphibians – flight attempts. I insisted that we only practise on inanimate test subjects from here on in, and Pooder reluctantly agreed. Mostly because he was despondent about the destruction of the drone, pieces of which we collected as we were hurrying to clean up the frog guts in the garden before Carol got to them so we could properly mourn and respectfully bury what was left of our late lamented aerodynamics test partner. But I couldn't help but notice that my father had more or less disappeared.

Of course not being a 'complete dolt' (borrowing again from Pooder's British phase) I had a pretty solid idea of what my dad was doing, especially since we noted he was spending a large amount of time going back and forth between Old Oscar's yard and his own workshop, and the sinking feeling in my gut was proof enough that it had to do with an upcoming bicycle for me.

I worried a bit when I saw the flash-glow of the wire-feed welder coming through the small windows. He had an uncanny ability to start unintentional fires with that welder. But no flames erupted, so I didn't bother him (but I did pull the refurbished fire extinguisher out from under the sink and had it ready just in case). And, again, given that our idea of time was as different as our take on high-living funds, I knew better than to count on him to create a bike in time to impress Peggy so there was no need to check his progress.

I focused instead on looking for a part-time job and wound up mowing a few lawns and cleaning out garages. But they didn't lead very far in terms of swift wealth accumulation, and when I tried getting work at some fast-food places, it turned out I was too young.

Pooder said that was outright age discrimination and we should organize a march. When I explained that two people didn't make much of an effective protest movement, he said we should post things on social media and the bulletin board at the super-market to get more people involved in lowering the legal hiring age at fast-food places.

I hated to point out, but I knew it wouldn't cross Pooder's mind, that if we undertook that endeav-our, I'd never become more accepted at school because then I'd be known as the maniac looking to undermine federal child labour laws. He looked so heartbroken at his flawed idea that I cheered him up by telling him that when I applied at the place where they deep-fry chicken, an employee on break out back of the place told me that it was too bad I wasn't going to get hired to work with him because then I'd never know how cool it was to dip something other than chicken in batter and stick it in hot grease. I shuddered to think what else he might have deep-fried and tried to put the whole thing from my mind, but Pooder immediately started making a list of possibilities given that I had met the fry guy in the alley by the dumpster.

Which is when I quit listening but not before coming to the decision that I probably wouldn't be eating much deep-fried fast food in the future, not that I ate much anyway (my dad, you know) whereupon (word from Pooder's phase when he thought he might become a high-priced lawyer or a Brit-forensic-scientist-slash-detective) Pooder said: 'We have to go back there.'

'And what Kentucky Fried reason would that be?'

'To find out what, exactly, he stuck in the grease.'

'Are you completely insane? Best-case scenario is that, while he didn't mean chicken, he was still in the realm of food because I'd heard about people who deep-fry chocolate bars and toaster pastries. Only he did not look like he had a sweet tooth, he looked like a worst-case-scenario guy who girls get warned about in PE class when they do self-defence. Believe me, you do not want to go back and try to finish *that* conversation.'

At which point Pooder stood up straight, took a deep breath, and flat-out pontificated (good word there, from when Pooder thought he might enter politics and give lots of speeches):

'You know what Socrates said.'

'Socrates?'

'Yeah. You know. The Greek philosopher. Born circa 470 BC or so—'

'Socrates? You're quoting Socrates?'

'Exactly. And the quote is, "The unexamined life is not worth living".'

He raised his finger in the air (probably holding a beat for the applause because he said that every good politician knew how to 'dangle the sound bite' – his phrase, not mine – and give the crowd a chance to roar its approval) and then held my gaze (eye contact being key to a trustworthy civil servant). 'So you absolutely need to go back and find out what this forward-thinking, deep-frying fast-food entrepreneur stuck in the hot grease because, you know, you absolutely don't want this information to become part of your unexamined life.'

'Still passing on that, Pooder. Absolutely.'

'Then the only other thing worth our time and energy is to find out what your dad is doing back in his shed.'

As if either of us didn't know exactly how my dad was 'working on' my request for a bike.

A BICYCLE FROM HELL

Of course there was never any doubt about how my dad was going to procure a bike for me. If it wasn't for Pooder, I probably wouldn't have pushed the envelope and – a few weeks after I gave him my wish list – asked my dad to show me what he'd been working on.

But Pooder was curious, and my dad said he'd been about to come get me anyway.

Using stuff from Old Oscar's junk piles, my father had been making me a bicycle with what Pooder calls his 'simply classic mission devotion and intense creative drive' and energy – instead of money – and put together what my dad called 'the bicycle to end all bicycles'.

Not 'a' bicycle but 'the' bicycle. I perked up a little there because I wanted to get 'the' girl and not 'a' girl with this new bike I was about to see.

As part of the lead-up to his reveal of the bike, Dad told us he had dug through Oscar's piles until he located 'the best of everything. I was looking for quality, boys, not just functionality'.

I had my doubts on that one, but I could tell that I stood alone in my opinion because Dad and Pooder were positively glowing at the unveiling of the finished product. Literally, an unveiling. My dad yanked a paint tarp off the finished product with what can only be called a flourish.

Pooder clapped.

My dad, I swear, wiped a tear away.

I bit my tongue and did some deep-breathing exercises.

'Even if you had the money to spend and bought all the parts brand-new instead of scrounging for free bits and then refurbishing them,' Pooder said, studying my dad's work, 'the end result might not have been half as impressive.'

'And this original creation,' my dad announced as he helped launch me on a wobbly test ride around our muddy excuse for a driveway, 'is of far superior quality to anything mass-produced for a bland herd of mindless consumers.'

Allow me to describe:

He had, indeed, found the best sealed-bearing hubs, 'so smooth and perfect that if the bike was upside down and you spun the front wheel, you could go off and eat lunch and when you came back, it would still be spinning,' Dad said.

I don't know why anyone would do that, but he and Pooder nodded approvingly as if that's the whole point of wheel bearings – endless unattended spinning.

The alloy pedals – with strapless metal toe clamps – also turned without any effort. 'So light they don't seem to be on your foot at all,' Pooder said, calling them 'air pedals', because they almost floated on the end of his feet when he jumped at the chance to switch places with me to 'get a feel for this beaut'.

The brushed aluminium alloy crank arms with three polished chainrings on the front and seven sprockets on the rear cassette clocked in with twenty-one possible gears.

'Anything,' Pooder said after halting his circles in our garden to shake my dad's hand and congratulate him on his efforts, 'you could possibly want or need, terrain-wise.'

The shifters for the front and rear gears were so smooth and lightning-fast it seemed the derailleurs could practically be shifted by thought alone. The wheel rims were of brushed aluminium, sturdy and only slightly corroded, with almost surgically balanced tension to the spokes, tires narrow and light enough for street racing but ample enough for gravel. And welds on the custom frame made from tubing cannibalized from a half-dozen junkyard frames had been done with such wire-feed-welder precision they seemed to not exist at all, smooth and seamless like the frame was created from one piece of liquid metal.

Have I mentioned the brakes? Not yet? Again,

exactly perfectly right disc brakes, so sensitive yet powerful they needed only a featherlight touch on the levers to bring the bike back to earth from space where it seemed almost to float when you rode it.

I'm aware that this description makes it sound like the perfect bike.

And it was.

Almost.

Because my father is the absolute monarch of the Kingdom of Almost-Was.

Only a few minor details – small things, infinitesimal things – kept this marvel of mechanical ingenuity and design perfection from being the bike of my dreams.

First of all, my dad had designed and built a recumbent bicycle.

Which is all right, in a way. Recumbents are fun and fast and they move right along. Unless you try going up a steep hill. All your power comes from your legs because you are essentially lying down, with your feet on pedals that stick over the front wheel, so you can't bring your body weight down on the pedals for added force to combat all that physics and angles and gravity stuff. That means pedalling uphill makes you sweat because you have to work harder. It's still okay because you can shift down to a lower gear and pedal faster for a lower speed up a potentially steep grade. So slow you might wobble a bit. But, still, you can get it done.

Did I mention my school is on a hill? A steep hill? Probably not. So, my dreams of gliding effort-lessly to the bike racks looking casual and chill were replaced with a nightmarish image of me flat on my back, pedalling madly but moving forward very slowly, hyperventilating, with leg cramps, semi-blinded from the sweat that, instead of rolling down my face all manly and Tour de France-like, is pooling in my eyes, stinging them and making them water so it looks like I've just had a good cry on my way to school.

Added to that pretty picture, a recumbent bike puts you roughly three feet lower than anybody standing near you and on a completely different plane of view from somebody who is riding a conventional bicycle.

And by 'anybody' and 'somebody', I mean, of course, Peggy. Who I have seen, like everyone else ever, riding a normal bike.

So, what my dad's hard work had ultimately provided was the opportunity for me to try to be accepted as a regular person by the best girl in middle school (not only my middle school, but quite possibly all middle schools everywhere over the entire history of middle schools), looking like an absolute dweeb on a homemade lie-down two-wheeler. 'Hi, up there,' I'd gasp, struggling and failing to sit upright (did I mention my body hates me and the parts that hate me most are my abs?). She would undoubtedly look around and after first seeing no one, eventually drop her gaze down to me, a semi-prone, self-propelled freaky perv pedalling around eye-level with people's bottoms and . . .

No.

Not a good way to start a relationship.

And to top it off, even if I somehow survived

what had been this attempt to make a good first impression – and what I should have mentioned before when I was going on about her hair and her eyes, was that Peggy's personality is aces, and she's supernaturally kind and may well have given me a pass for the weird style of biped – but then my father went and added the final touch, the crowning glory:

The seat.

Which, in reality and, if you ask me, quite beside the point, was extremely comfortable. He'd made it of beautifully welded pipe with exactly the right lean-back angle, and the front edge brought my legs up so my feet hit the pedals exactly right.

Perfect.

But remember now, I told you this already, my father leans well into the concept of being practical and has never been one to honour the cosmetic side of things. Looks, for him, came in a distant second place during his design process and while the seat was comfortable and fit me exactly right . . .

He had covered it with a plastic-laminated, crinkly

upholstery of huge palm fronds and garish flamingos that he had apparently lifted off an old lounge chair from one of Oscar's piles. It had probably been on the edge of somebody's pool for many summers because the flamingos were no longer that vibrant, screaming, pinky-orange colour, but a light dusty pink. And the fronds had faded from a jungle green to a light moss, making the whole pattern look gently floral, rather than robustly tropical.

'It looks like the weird sofa thing my grandfather sits on in the all-season porch when he gets some sun at the assisted-living home,' Pooder said, 'only with wheels.' He gazed happily at the bike sitting there in the sun, propped up on what must have been a Harley kickstand.

Dad had painted the frame black. Not sprayed and glossy, but flat-black paint applied with what must have been a coarse brush, so in some places the original colour of the parts, and sometimes rust, showed through. Sort of spotted. Like it had some disease – call it bicycle leprosy – and the flatness of the paint seemed to absorb light. I blinked, trying to clear my vision but nope. When the light hit the paint just right, it produced an optical illusion that shimmered and looked like the portal to a new time-space continuum.

I could not even begin to imagine riding the bike to school, or the shopping centre, or anywhere. Pedalling along, absorbing light, causing a porta-ble, miniature black hole wherever I went, coming up next to and well below Peggy like a mysterious lurking shadow and giving a hearty greeting to her behind.

It was, simply, not acceptable.

The bike, that is.

And something, clearly, had to be done.

About my father, that is.

A POSSIBLE SOLUTION INVOLVING PUPPIES

I initially considered that I could perhaps run away from home, and I gave it serious thought for a while (and, by 'a while', I mean as I pictured myself riding this bike to school) as a way to avoid my dad and his philosophies and ways of looking at life that make everything harder than it has to be for me.

I could run somewhere, out West, probably, and get a job on a ranch that paid actual money rather than stuff like bags of rice and dried beans that my dad thinks is the greatest payday of his life.

The ranch work would make me strong and allow me to save up a pile of money of my own and then, eventually, I'd come back all tanned and tall and bronzed and probably without needing glasses anymore and my abs would be rock-hard and I'd accidentally run into Peggy and then . . .

I snapped myself out of that line of thinking before I said anything out loud because Pooder would have teased me like crazy for how 'barking mad' I was (another term from his British phase).

Plus, he loved the bike, thought the whole situation was nothing short of hilarious, and took to calling it 'your nursing home Harley'.

'The best thing about it,' he said, 'is that it makes you look older. More mature. About seventy-five. Ride the bike long enough and you'll probably be covered with wrinkles, trying to pull coins out of everyone's ears like my grandfather, only everyone at the assisted-living home is onto him and they stay an arm's length away now and he doesn't get to watch his shows if he doesn't observe and respect people's personal space, which he says is nothing more or less than an unhealthy dislike of magic tricks.'

'Quit messing around, Pooder. This is serious. Whatever it is that makes my dad so . . . dad-like seems to be getting worse all the time. Last night at dinner he told me he's now considering reweaving old cloth and sewing our own clothes because he says they did it in prehistory, before they even understood the concept of money. Can you imagine me heading for school riding this . . . this . . . supine rolling lawn-chair Death Star thing wearing hand-stitched clothes made of woven scrap cloth?'

Pooder has this smile. I've talked about it before – this strange little quirky smile that makes you not sure if he's kidding because what he says always sounds so far-fetched and unreasonable but the way he says it is always so certain. Anyway, he was smiling that smile now.

'You're looking at this all wrong,' he told me. 'What we do, see, is we get a video of you in your new clothes on your new bike. I can use my phone to film you even though it's not that good at motion. A little fuzzy. Still, I'm thinking that we throw that sucker on the internet. I already have a channel, just lacking quality content, you know. As soon as we get that video loaded, we'll rack up viewing numbers and then we can make some coin when the big corporations start to want to advertise on it.'

'You don't say.'

'I do say. I see stuff like this all the time. I've made a study of self-made social media phenoms. You know, if I pitch it right . . .'

One of Pooder's phases that, to be fair, he kept drifting in and out of, unlike the other fair-weather ideas, was his dream to form a company. He's never very detailed about what kind of company or how he'd start one, but he did work up the design for his business card and made a list of necessary office supplies, including an adjustable standing desk with a balance ball chair and adjoining treadmill attachment 'to maximize both work efficiency and physical fitness'. He plans to make a lot of money as an agent or adman ('Are they the same thing,' he asked once, 'or would I be the first agent/adman hybrid?'), pitching ideas (he tries to remember to carry around a notebook for jotting down these pitchable ideas, only he keeps losing them – the notebooks and then the ideas) and stacking coin.

'Pooder—'

'I can see it now. We start with you off in the distance, so you're just a black dot, and then lay in some music as you come closer until you stop right in front of the camera and you say—'

'Knock it off.'

'No. Not that. You'll say something like, "Hi, everything I'm wearing and riding is made completely of recycled material," and that will lock up the green and eco-friendly market as well as the global corporations who only want to appeal to a young demographic and are always looking for convincing influencers to partner up with because today's youth is tomorrow's consumer or the hope for the future or whatever.'

'Are you done yet?'

'Never. But I can see that your mind is elsewhere. The dad thing. So, what are you going to do?'

'I am open to suggestions. But only good ones.'

The thing with Pooder is, kidding aside, when

there is a real problem, he is a ride-or-die friend and won't stop until he helps you out of the jam you're in. Perhaps because of what he calls his fertile imagination, his brain works like the best kind of artificial intelligence. There's logic, observational ability, and, oddly enough, a good portion of common sense stacked up behind that quirky mind and filterless mouth. I looked at him hopefully.

'I don't have a thing,' he said. 'Not a blessed thing.'

'I was not expecting that from you, to be honest.'

'The problem is your dad is too good. He thinks all the time and really cares about you. I would kill to have your dad. Lately, mine comes home from work, pours a glass of what he calls his nighttime wine – red, because white wine is for the day and red for the night – clicks on the television, works his way through the bottle, and then goes to bed. I don't think he's said four words to me or my mom this week. I'm not even sure he remembers our names. Your dad actually talks to you, seems to like you and care what you say or do. The ideal father, except . . .'

'Except what?'

'Well . . .'

'He's crazy, right?'

Pooder shook his head. 'Not at all. He's obviously a genius. It's just that he has a completely unique way of looking at things—'

'His way.'

Pooder nodded. 'Exactly. He sees things not as they are, but as they could be in the best of situations.'

'Just not necessarily my way.'

'True.'

'So what do I do?'

'Elementary, my dear Watson.' (Pooder's British phase included, but was not limited to, him wanting to be a detective like Sherlock Holmes for a while, and he still enjoyed the opportunity to misquote Sir Arthur Conan Doyle, who, he informed me, never wrote such a line.)

'Enlighten me.'

'You have to reboot your father.'

There it was. Simple, clean.

'You're stuck with a really good guy who just needs some tweaks in the father department. You're going to have to change him to be something you can live with. Or something with which you can live.'

Pooder started paying attention to grammar rules after Ms Johnson, our English teacher last year, had what he called a glow-up and Pooder thought if he grew up and became an English teacher they might meet at a teacher's convention and . . . well, let's just say I'm not the only one with hopes that may not be realistic.

'And how do I reboot my dad?'

'Not a clue.' Pooder shook his head, then shrugged. 'It's not like you can turn him off for ten or fifteen seconds and then turn him back on and he'll self-adjust to what you want, like a laptop. I only know the what, I do not know the how.'

But it was there, right there, that fate kicked in and took over.

Often you can't tell when that is in life, don't see it until it's in the past, but that time, at that juncture (a word again from when Pooder walked around saying things like 'whereas at this juncture the plaintiff made known his aforementioned predilection for wasting his efforts on . . .'), fate made its move, presenting me with what I thought might become a solution.

Puppies.

Dramatic pause.

I can tell right now that you might be a little skeptical in thinking that puppies can solve this thing. It's not like I went out and adopted a litter of puppies to distract my father from his philosophies, although there is something about a pile of puppies that can be pretty distracting. A pile of puppies is way cuter than a basket of baby ducks, which I think is measurably cuter than a pile of kittens on a table covered with balls of yarn, and I wonder if Peggy likes puppies . . .

Got sidetracked there. Sorry.

Pooder caught it. He's reading this as I go and he's worried that I'm addled and might lose my commitment and mind in a fortnight. (He's working now at being a writer in Victorian England. Between us, he had to look up the word *fortnight* before he used it because he initially thought it might be something about a military installation after dark.)

So I was talking to Pooder and he had the what but not the how to handle my dad problem, and that's when fate stepped in. Because that's when I looked up at the wall and saw the colour calendar that is sent free each year from the feed shop where we buy hog and chicken feed and – here is the stroke of puppy genius – dog food.

Just a run-of-the-mill freebie calendar with generic pictures of baby calves and ducklings and chicks. They might switch it up from month to month and throw in a barn, a covered bridge, a mountain range with snowy peaks, and even a pretty girl wearing a plaid shirt and dungarees chewing on a piece of straw while she looks out across a farm field. But mainly it was baby animals.

And this month featured a photograph of a distractingly cute pile of husky puppies.

Which reminded me of a recent purchase at the shop.

That's where fate was hiding. That's where fate showed me where to look for the how.

In a forty-two-pound bag of dry dog food.

You weren't there, so let me explain.

See, we couldn't leave bags of dog food out in the open because Carol might have been related to a chainsaw and there was probably some blood-hound in her family tree, too, and she was always up for a snack, even if she had just eaten. If you left the bag of dog food out, she'd find it and shred it and tear it apart like she did with skunks and then try to eat it. Like she did with skunks.

But forty-two pounds of dry dog food is a chal-lenge even for a pit bull like her. She'd eat until she couldn't hold any more, then puke it up and then eat more – puke, eat, puke, eat, puke. And, because she was feminine and oddly delicate with good man-ners and a strong sense of pride about her garden, she was always careful to puke where it wouldn't mess up the garden. She'd run for the trailer, climb the three steps, and puke on the porch.

'She wants to share it,' Pooder said the first time

he saw Carol's worst trick. 'She's so cute.'

'That's because you don't have to clean it up,' I said, scooping up piles of dog vomit – wondering why it turned into green-yellow goober snot after it went through her mouth and stomach – with an old shovel we kept for picking up pieces of shredded skunk.

After a couple of what we call the puke-and-rally incidents, we figured out that the bag had to be opened and the contents poured into a metal rubbish bin with a tight lid to keep Carol out of it. Earlier that day, I'd carried a new sack into the shed, opened the top of the metal barrel, ripped the sack open, and poured the food down into the bottom.

Except this wasn't Carol's usual brand of dog food. It was a giant sack of puppy chow, which Dad had found on the markdown shelf at the feed shop, owing to a tear in the corner of the bag. The damage had been taped over and the bag looked fine otherwise, so it seemed a bargain find of Dad's that made sense to me. As I'd emptied it into the bin that morning, I'd seen that the dog food company had put a small pamphlet inside the sack.

It had poured out and was almost completely hidden under the dog food, but I saw the corner of it and grabbed it. Usually those things are just advertisements or coupons for other products they sell, like collars or chew toys. I rarely read or even look at them too carefully and I barely glanced at it as I shoved it in my pocket to recycle later.

I'd caught a glimpse of the text, though, enough to realize now that fate was nudging me hard, and I pulled it out of my pocket and looked down.

The pamphlet had a sketch of a puppy on the cover. The print under the picture read:

TRAINING YOUR PUPPY USING POSITIVE REINFORCEMENT

See?

Fate.

The how part of my dad problem was, literally, in my hands.

TRAINING YOUR PUPPY

Positive puppy training is all about rewarding good behaviour. And ignoring bad behaviour. All training efforts should be subtle and positive; under no circumstance should you yell or scold or angrily rub a puppy's nose in its mess. So states the first sentences of the pamphlet.

All right, I know my father isn't a puppy and that there are some pretty glaring differences between my father and said puppy.

But are there really?

My father is a mammal and a puppy is a mammal, and according to science, there are very few differences in the DNA of all mammals.

In fact, I think I read (or, more likely my dad or

Pooder read and then told me as an aside of some long drawn-out story) that there is only supposed to be a seventeen- or eighteen-chromosome difference between humans and lawn grass.

And I think in some cases – as with Pooder – it might even be a little closer.

Not that I could use the pamphlet to train lawn grass, although I did read (or, again, Pooder or my dad may have told me) that if you mow down dandelions in your garden, the plant that's left never grows above the height of the mower blade again. So if a person can train a dandelion to keep its head down and duck underneath a mower, it seems like you could probably train lawn grass. Not to do your taxes or anything like that, but maybe to keep it from coming up through the cracks in the sidewalk –

Well. Got off on another sidetrack there. Again, sorry, and thanks to Pooder for slowing me down (because if that factory-made-meat-loving thing of his hasn't rubbed off on me, his propensity for conversational tangents sure has).

When I told Pooder of my idea – which was to use the puppy training methods to alter my father's unwanted behaviours – he couldn't help himself and went off on the humourous point of view rather than appreciating the practical aspect.

'So if you catch your father chewing one of your shoes, you can use positive reinforcement to make him stop? How about if your father starts chasing cars? What if you catch your father pooping on the rug?'

'Pooder.'

'Or if he starts jumping up on people and ruining their clothes—'

'That's enough.'

'Not really. I've got a million of them. What about if your father starts humping—'

'If you don't stop this instant, I will post the Mountain of Doom video.'

I was referring to a truly embarrassing (to him) but delightful (to me) video where he was wearing an old army surplus helmet and a too-large moth-eaten flight jacket making engine-revving noises while pretending to be a fighter pilot rescuing the girl held on the mountaintop by the evil villain who happens to be near an airstrip on what you call the Mountain of Doom. He called it 'method inventing' and swore it made his ideas more realistic. He had been working on a new video game that he was certain would make him a pile of coin. He didn't know I had my phone on action video when he did it. The video has been handy. I've successfully used it as a threat several times.

'You wouldn't.'

'I certainly will.'

'So' – he tried to be serious, but I could see it was a strain on him – 'you're going to positively reinforce him when he does something wrong and not punish him if he goes poopy on the floor—'

'Pooder.'

'Well, that's how it seems to me. You can't be serious about this.'

'This from a guy who quotes Socrates as reason to cosy up to the deranged chef who may or may not routinely stick non-FDA-approved items in the hot grease at a restaurant open to and serving the general public.'

'Well, who would you quote?'

'Seriously, if you look at what they're saying in the pamphlet, it seems like with a little modification the techniques could work.' Hopeful voice, I thought, but it may have been the tone of pleading. And I guess I was. 'Like you said before, I can't run away. I'm too young, plus he's too good a father for me to do that – I don't want to hurt his feelings.'

'So, positive reinforcement. Got it. What do you do when he does something right?'

'"When"?'

'Well, all right. *If.* If he does something right?'

'According to the pamphlet, you praise him.'

'And if he does something wrong?'

'Not wrong. Just incorrect. And not if, but when. And that's a definite – when he does something incorrect. Because he will. This I know.'

'How will you know to judge what's right or wrong, sorry, incorrect?'

'I think it will come to me.'

'And what do you do then?'

'According to the pamphlet, you don't do anything, you ignore it and don't praise him.'

'What if that doesn't work?'

'I haven't read the whole pamphlet yet.'

'I see.' Pooder sighed. 'Maybe, since you're kind of altering a whole human life – sorry, mammalian life – you ought to read the entire instruction booklet before you set about housebreaking your father.'

'You don't believe this has the slightest chance of working, do you?'

'Not a whit.' Another gem from Pooder's British phase. I was certain he didn't know what it meant, but he did come up with a nice variety of usable British swear words – *bloody* and *sod off* were particular favourites.

'But,' he added, 'I'm going to keep an audio-visual journal of your whole experiment to study later. Maybe use it for a documentary. Might be a chance to pick up some coin if I could get it distributed by one of the streaming platforms. Do you think there's any chance your dad'll sue?'

Sometimes Pooder jumping from phase to phase without warning can be a little confusing. He might start things off an English lord before suddenly becoming an advertising mogul looking to make some coin and then turn into a Viking biting deep on a tomato-apple so the juice runs down into his beard-if-he-had-one while he's thinking of pillaging a coast somewhere. Whenever he goes that way, I lean back until he's done or at least settles in on just one phase at a time.

I ignored his latest career-path idea, but I did grab an old notebook. He'd made a good point about tracking the success and failure of the experiment; I'd have to take careful notes, see what worked. Luckily, an opportunity to test the training theory on my dad presented itself almost immediately.

A garage sale.

THE GARAGE SALE

As Pooder would be happy to explain, the concept of a 'garage sale' is simple and it does not mean anyone's trying to sell you their garage. What they do, see, is that people who have a lot of junk in their lives that they don't want any longer drag it out of the basement or attic or closet and put it out on boxes and tables and chairs in front of their homes, or in their open garages, and try to sell it to people who come along and are suckers enough to pay good money for it.

My dad would, of course, replace the operable words of *junk* and *suckers* with the kinder verbiage of *reusables* and *bargain-hunters*.

We've been going to garage sales forever; he

likes them only slightly less than he adores Oscar's yard. He got Pooder hooked, too. I used to like poking around with Dad until I got a little older and his garage-sale finds started to impact my life, and not for the better.

As we've already discussed, he finds value in things that other people don't quite understand.

For instance, dungarees.

He thinks they are the most practical thing in the world when it comes to apparel. He sees them as comfortable with a lot of handy pockets and made of tough fabric that will last a long time.

A long time, as far as I can tell at twelve going on thirteen, means 'forever'.

So when he went to a garage sale and found a couple pairs of dungarees that would fit me, he offered to change the oil in the lady's leaky car in the driveway for them and brought them home for me to wear. They were like new and well washed and he considered them a major bartering coup and a huge leap forward in the matter of practical clothing for a growing boy.

'You can wear them every day. You know, for messing around or dog-puke cleaning up. Good pockets to carry anything you need. Comfortable.'

Which was all fine and well. Only . . .

The dungarees had originally belonged to a female. And while it was true they fit me and might be nice for what Dad called 'everyday walking-around wear', they were more of a style statement for a fashion-forward young woman than a utilitarian knockabout piece of clothing for a guy who's trying to become lookatable material in the good way.

There were words, cute and flirtatious words such as QUEEN BEE and HOT STUFF, written on patches randomly sewn all over the overalls. Even after I pulled off the patches and washed the dungarees, Pooder pointed out that the ink had leached through and permanently stained the denim itself.

'It would take an enormous amount of personal confidence to wear a pair of pink dungarees with the words SWEET CHEEKS written across the butt, no matter how faded, even for fishing and drone work in the yard,' he said, obviously sad to agree with me that this particular dad moment was an inarguable fail.

Did I forget to mention they were pink?

But my father saw nothing wrong with them. All he could see was that it was a major bartering coup and didn't I, after all was said and done, need work overalls?

If only the dungarees were the beginning and end of my dad's garage-sale discoveries . . .

Every garage sale seems to have one common feature – old video cameras and VHS tapes of movies that were older than dirt. The broken video cameras were right in the middle of my father's wheelhouse when it came to fixing things, and while he felt that general television was pretty awful and nothing on the internet was worth watching, videotapes of movies where the actors had died of old age before I was born were impossible for him to resist.

He particularly enjoyed murder mystery movies set before DNA was known so the detective had to more or less go by hunches when it came to solving crimes. And any good science-fiction films, according to my dad, were filmed in black and white with cardboard cutouts of the monsters and aliens. My father firmly believed these films were 'classics', like the truck or sump pump, and he could not walk away from them. And, of course, he had to salvage and repair the old video players so these classics could be played.

Imagine this: me, in a pair of pink dungarees covered with cutesy faded sayings, like SWEETIE PIE and OH YOU DARLING, and a T-shirt screen-printed with the crooked slogan DALLAS TIRE REPAIR AND WING SHACK (Dad scored an entire box of those because the logo was wonky), wearing a pair of high-top black-and-white-canvas trainers only one size too large ('you'll grow into them soon enough') and a large straw hat with a green visor on the front edge held on by a chin strap made of frayed orange baler twine, toting several boxes of VHS tapes and a couple video machines back to the truck, while my dad changed out the storm windows on the back porch in an even trade.

Oh, how I came to hate garage sales once the idea

of becoming lookatable to Peg was on my mind.

But it was at one of the weekly garage sales Dad dragged me to that fate – remember fate? – once again kicked in and set up the first real test of my positive-reinforcement father-training experiment.

We were on our way back from town, just the three of us sitting across the seat in the truck, Dad, Carol, and me. Carol loved to go to town, to ride in the truck and stare intensely out the front as we drive – my father says she's cataloguing potential prey items, looking for any possible security threats to what's hers. Her favourite moments are when she spies a garage sale.

The reason Carol gets so excited is that my father becomes a predator when he spots a garage sale and she reacts to it, enters into the pack mentality, triggers on my dad's right eye, where dogs always look for human emotions. (True fact, which I learned from Pooder. Check it out on your dog if you've got one. If you don't, go get one. Pooder says nobody can live completely without a dog in their life even though his father won't let him have one. Get a rescue dog and you'll save more than only the dog. You'll save yourself. Pooder says so and he's only wrong 26.5 per cent of the time. Good odds.)

The prey – tables stacked with stuff – sit waiting in summer heat.

We drive carefully past to see what sort of sale it is.

'Don't give away that we're interested,' my father says like always, and Carol picks up on his warning, watching the sale like a cheetah looking at a herd of antelope, no direct eye contact, careful study-but-not-study as we drive past.

The rules of the hunt are simple.

Look, but don't let them see we're looking.

No buying sight unseen – this after the time we stopped at one sale with a stack of sealed cardboard boxes and Dad was too curious not to get out and make an offer then and there because someone else was eyeing the boxes and his predator instinct got the best of him. Only to find out when we opened the box at home that it was stinky and mouldy whipped-cream and cottage-cheese and sour-cream containers, which was not only a disgusting bummer in the moment, but forever put us off dairy.

Think practical. The correct procedure was to look for gently broken tools he could fix or good used kitchen utensils, work boots that might almost fit, and any quality athletic or leisure gear that might be a bargain. The everyday necessities that other people buy at shopping centres with their hard-earned ertogs. (We once almost got a two-person kayak, but were outbid by some guy who was willing to pay cash, and not just clean the garage-sale guy's gutters.)

Give potential purchases a careful inspection. Another time we thought we had scored on a recliner that seemed perfect. Not until we got it home did we discover that we had also purchased a family of rats that had built a nest in the springs under the seat cushion – a reeking collection of cotton upholstery stuffing, sticks, grass, and, judging by the smell, urine to glue it all together. Since rats make more rats, at a frighteningly speedy rate, Dad says, and he is a live-and-let-live kind of guy, we dragged the chair back outside and let them keep it.

During today's initial drive-by of the potential garage sale, I was thinking about that chair and its family of rats and how Dad never really paid any attention to his own garage-sale rules. That's when I decided it was time to apply a technique I'd picked up from the puppy-training pamphlet.

The basic idea seemed simple: ignore bad behaviour and praise good behaviour.

Since the 'dog' (who I began referring to as 'SP' for *Subject Puppy* because Pooder said it would sound more experimental and official that way when I wrote down accounts of my training efforts in my notebook at night) was starting to do something inappropriate, I practised ignoring SP and his bad behaviour.

I didn't want to let SP think I was interested in what SP might be doing and thereby call attention to SP.

SPs crave attention.

I quickly discovered that it's a little hard to ignore something your SP and killer dog are staring-but-not-staring at, as you're casually driving back and forth in front of someone's house, trying to study-not-study the items in the driveway, especially when SP is busy driving the truck that's carrying you.

But I tried.

I pretended to nonchalantly look out the opposite side window of the truck, away from the prey object/potential garage-sale stop, and tried to appear wildly interested in a bird that was flying overhead.

Carol fell for it and looked where I was pointing. When she realized it was an ordinary, boring bird and that I'd diverted her attention away from Dad's garage-sale hunt for nothing, she looked deep into my eyes – I got the distinct impression she knew exactly what I was doing and did not approve – and then went back to her job of studying-not-studying the sale with my dad.

SP didn't even glance up at the bird. As we drove past, I could see him fixate on a beat-up rusty rowing machine. Then he shook his head and muttered to himself, 'Nah.'

We picked up speed and I thought we were free

and clear. It seemed a perfect moment for some positive reinforcement. 'Good thinking,' I said. (I almost said, 'Good boy.') 'Didn't seem like there was much of anything there.'

SP didn't respond, and as we made a series of left turns to swing past the garage sale again, I understood that he wasn't giving up so easily. As we passed by a second time, he perked up. 'I think I see an electric hedge trimmer we might be able to make use of.'

He then drove around the block again, pulled up to the curb in front of the sale, and went directly to the trimmer, which he bargained down to two dollars, and bought. (SP barters if the amount is over ten bucks, but anything under five and he pays cash, a crumpled single and spare change in this case.) Considering that we didn't have anything that even remotely resembled a hedge or any other kind of topiary achievement except the four scrawny trees, it seemed a waste of two dollars.

SP and Carol spent the next two hours – two hours of my life that I will never get back – looking for other so-called bargains and chatting with other customers because they are my dad's kindred spirits, while I sat in the truck looking out the window away from the sale ignoring SP's inappropriate behaviour. I ignored my dog's inappropriate behaviour, too (Carol had her own form of shopping that most people call shoplifting).

Using the 'ignoring bad behaviour/positive reinforcement' routine didn't seem to have any appreciable effect whatsoever.

SP had still worked the garage sale and bought something we didn't need and Carol had stolen a stuffed bunny.

They had ignored me ignoring them and did not stop their bad behaviour in order to seek my attention.

My first attempt at training SP was a complete and utter failure.

STEP TWO

'But was it really?'

Pooder and I were sitting down by the river after my first attempt to train my dad. I was dejected. 'Complete and utter failure,' I had written in my SP experiment notebook, which I was annoyed to admit fit perfectly in the front pocket of my pink dungarees.

'How do you call it a failure?'

'He went for the garage sale anyway,' I answered. 'I gave him some positive reinforcement when he seemed to be giving up on the sale. When he didn't, I ignored the peewadden out of him and the whole business of the garage sale and he jumped out anyway and started – well, bargaining – and the procedure didn't work at all. I even tried to distract him with a bird. Didn't even look. Total failure.'

'Once,' Pooder said.

'What?'

'You did it once, one measly time, and even then it was mainly about being negative. You think a puppy would quit peeing or pooping on the floor after you ignore him once? You need to keep trying, give it another chance.'

'I thought you didn't believe in any of this.'

'Well, I guess I don't. But if you're going to try it, really work at this experiment, then I feel you should at least give it a serious effort. Am I, for instance, going to give up on the frog-altitude experiment? No. No, I will not. No matter the cost in time and effort, I will stay with it until we break the record.'

'I don't think frogs like record-breaking altitude experiments. Well, at least not the first frog.' We paused to look down and cover our hearts in memory. 'I bet if he, the first frog, had been asked, he would just as soon have stayed on the ground. Made it a jumping contest.'

'Already been done,' Pooder said with heaping scorn. 'The record books are full of stories about jumping frogs. Nothing about altitude. And except for that little glitch when the harness slipped it would have been perfect.'

'He dropped and splatted all over. It was gross and really sad. Asking another frog to risk his life would be cruel.'

'Well, that's not the point.' Pooder changed the subject. 'The point here is to alter your father's *approach* – for lack of a better word – his *approach* to living and problem solving. And one chance encounter is not enough.'

And, of course, he was right. As we've discussed, he often is right. Unfortunately, when he's wrong it can sometimes be catastrophic – like trying to get a frog to go where no frog has gone before or getting a wooden hoe handle across his backside as a Viking in a tomato patch.

But mistakes aside, there was something to what Pooder said.

The problem was, summer was the season for garage sales. And while going from one garage sale to the next gave me a lot of opportunities to use the new procedure on an old behaviour that I wanted to break him of, I couldn't figure out how to factor in better positive reinforcement.

So I dutifully continued going with him, trying to find ways to introduce positive reinforcements and hoping he'd pick up on the being ignored part. Which I was not even that good at, to be honest.

He came loping back to the truck at the next garage sale holding an old attaché case made of scuffed plastic-leather with the name CARLYLE written on the side in gold letters.

'For carrying your schoolwork. Look, your books and homework will fit inside of it with plenty of room for a sandwich or banana.'

'But,' I said, unable to keep ignoring SP and despite my best intentions to deprive him of attention, 'my name isn't Carlyle.'

He shrugged. 'It doesn't matter. Your uncle Henry had a dog named Carlyle so it's like a family name. You can use it.'

I did manage to hold my tongue when he dropped a giant clear bin bag containing wrapped bundles of pink washcloths in the truck after the next garage-sale stop. I didn't even ask, but that didn't stop him from bragging, 'One hundred and seventy-five of them. They make perfect little towels.' I also didn't say a word even after I found the hygienic challenge of wiping myself dry with an eight-by-eight-inch towel after my next shower to be very involving.

At the next garage sale, and the next, SP not only didn't notice my silence and adjust his incorrect behaviour to once again seek my attention, he seemed to thrive on being ignored. Because: one hundred and fourteen individually packaged new toothbrushes. Or, as Pooder put it, 'One for each tooth for the rest of your life.' And then: thirty-two 3XL camouflage T-shirts. 'You can use them for camo-tents,' Pooder said. 'Sit inside hiding while eating your sandwich and banana out of your briefcase and brushing each tooth. Seriously, Carlyle, I think you're being too picky.'

I kept folding T-shirts while he was talking. SP had learned from a woman at a previous garage sale how to fold shirts like little burritos so they stood up neatly in the dresser drawer. It was oddly soothing.

But something had to be done. Clearly.

Before I started answering to Carlyle.

Time to read the rest of the pamphlet.

ROLLING IN THE GRASS

Pooder says I should copy down exactly what the pamphlet says, but I'm going to keep paraphrasing what I took away from it (Pooder says that's annotating the original text; I'm not sure that means what he thinks it means, but he's being a lot of help here, so . . .).

My next takeaway: Use distraction. According to the pamphlet, if a pup persists in incorrect behaviour, it is sometimes necessary to suddenly replace said behaviour by distracting the pup with something pup will enjoy doing. For example, throwing a ball or Frisbee, romping in the woods or at a dog park, rolling on his back in the grass. The pamphlet suggested I needed to get down on the ground and roll around with my puppy-in-training.

That sounded good. So I tried. Not rolling in the grass. But I did start carrying a tennis ball in the truck and, the following weekend, when my dad pulled up at a garage sale, I jumped out and engaged him in a game of catch right there on a stranger's front lawn.

Or tried to engage him in a game of catch.

'All right!' I said the first time he caught the ball, as if he'd just made a game-winning catch at the wall in centre field.

But all my positive exclamations only worked for a couple of tosses before the lure of the sale pulled his focus and he looked past me and saw a dinged-up bread machine and he was gone.

Flat gone, before I even caught the ball he'd thrown at me.

I didn't think taking him to the park or rolling around on the grass (and we didn't even *have* grass, it's only mud outside the trailer) would work, and since the throwing-a-ball idea was a no go, I turned to the pamphlet again that evening.

Then two things kicked in, which might not be

fate but are so close to it I'm calling it fate anyway.

Considering what came to pass, Pooder wants me to tell you it was Operation Outright Cowardice, but I think that's a little strong.

When we got home that afternoon I sat down with the pamphlet, read it again (Pooder says I need to confess that I only skimmed parts of it), and then tried to write in my experiment notebook, in my own words and in a very calculating manner focused on my own SP, rather than the generic and obviously much easier-to-train puppies the pamphlet was talking about, what should come next.

Carl: Try treats on SP!

The pamphlet said if the distraction procedure didn't work at first, you should tabulate other things you think your pup would like and substitute them when bad behaviour surfaced, alternating them so they do not become boring.

Something bad, something good, something bad . . .

However, the pamphlet went on to say that if

one desirable positive behaviour becomes manifest (Pooder says I should write *manifest* here because it is a fancier word than *common*), it was all right to concentrate on encouraging that one behaviour.

Enter Dairy Queen, stage left, moving full speed ahead to centre stage.

But first, a pause.

A pause for paws, and I'm sorry for the pun but Pooder says that when humour comes along like that you have to go with it. 'Humour's a lot like fate that way,' he added. 'Opportunities to notice and enjoy things that are perfect are very rare and you have to pay attention and then jump on them.'

The pause for paws has to do with Carol.

I read in an article on dogs in some scientific book (okay, so my dad or Pooder read it and told me about it later, but I remember the facts clear enough as if I had read it myself) that the smartest dogs were border collies, that they were so smart it was sometimes difficult for people to stay ahead of them. The book described the case of a woman with a year-old border collie pup who came home after a day away to find her kitchen entirely filled with sheep. Only she did not own any sheep, and even if she did, she probably wouldn't keep them in the kitchen. She later found out that the dog went to a nearby farm, on his own, opened the gates, 'borrowed' the sheep, herded the flock back to his house, opened the door to the house, and put the sheep in the kitchen. Because he didn't have any sheep of his own and probably thought that was sad but was smart enough to come up with a solution and steal himself a few sheep.

Which is some crazy-smart dog, even the lady with the sheep in her kitchen admitted that much, and she had to deal with all the wee and poop from the sheep on her kitchen floor.

Good article. But then it went on to claim that pit bulls were not that bright, at least not border collie bright.

Turns out they're wrong. Dead wrong.

What happened is that Carol started to smell a rodent, if not a rat like the ones that were living in the garage-sale recliner, then a pretty big mouse.

About the third time I tried to keep SP away from a garage sale, I caught Carol looking intently into my right eye, the seat of human emotions, and a cheat sheet, if you will, for smart dogs trying to figure out their people.

We were sitting in the truck making the first pass on the new sale when I noticed her staring into my eye, studying me. She knew something strange was going on, and by the time I had attempted to distract my dad from two more sales that day (Pooder says I need to tell you that it's possible to go from sale to sale every weekend all summer long, which of course drove me right up the wall), she had pretty much figured things out.

Not completely, but she knew, sensed, that I was trying to keep my father away from garage sales and deprive her of the opportunity to do a bit of shoplifting. And while she didn't know exactly why, the fact that I was interfering with the whole garage-sale dynamic was enough to make her skeptical of my intentions.

She loved hitting garage sales with SP, felt

herself a true comrade in arms with him, and obviously believed they shared the pack mentality, I guess, so anything (that would be me) that got between her and her pack leader when they were hot on the trail of prey – in this case, garage-sale bargains and dog thievery – doubled her suspicion.

And your suspicious pit bull is your alarming pit bull.

The next time I tried to distract SP from a sale, I felt a nudge on my thigh, and I turned to face Carol.

She was smiling at me.

I choose to call it smiling, but the truth was she was displaying an absolutely extraordinary amount of ivory.

It seemed like her whole head was made of teeth.

Add to the teeth, a deeply chilling sound.

Not a growl, exactly. More a gurgling, throaty whine, a mixture of eagerness and threat, like she would hate to have to go completely medieval on me but if it had to happen she wouldn't altogether mind.

The sound, combined with the display of teeth, made my spine go soft and the little hairs on the back of my neck stand up. I had been reaching for the door handle to get out and try to lead SP away from the sale, which I had done previously, but Carol looked at my hand, smiled, and then peered intently into my right eye while extending the claws on her paw that had been resting on my thigh until she nearly drew blood. I dropped my hand away from the handle. I swear she nodded her approval.

In the interests of staying alive and unmaimed – I've seen Carol crunch a small board in two with one bite when she's just playing – I headed back to the pamphlet for more feedback and additional training ideas.

It was important, according to the pamphlet, that if the SP – and presumably SP's semi-weaponized pit bull – did not respond to the distract/substitute principle, you should use a shock treatment of intense positive reinforcement to regain SP's attention before continuing in a more subtle way. Pick something SP loved to do and try it for a relief period.

And there were few things my father liked better than Dairy Queen, the one place guaranteed to get him to dig into his pocket without first asking if he could trade some handyman work for a couple of milkshakes and a cone for the dog. He almost enjoyed spending money at the DQ and I was all about capitalizing on what worked. If I could get him in the habit of frequently spending money on delicious ice cream, it would be a quick leap or a slippery slope to other purchasing endeavours.

Happily, but not surprisingly, Carol was of a like mind. Perhaps her favourite treat in the whole world — next to shredding a skunk that's bent upon killing our wandering chickens — was taking a whole Dairy Queen cone in her mouth and then squeezing her jaws shut around it. *Squeeze* might not be the right word. It was more of a chomp — a gleeful two-thousand, six-hundred pounds per square inch, lightning-slam chomp — on a defenceless Dairy Queen cone, which projectile-squirted vanilla ice cream through her lips so she could joyously, slowly, lick clean her drippy muzzle and sticky nose.

I had discovered yet another training tool, thank you to the good folks at DQ, and I began to use it at once.

And it worked well.

For a time.

Loosely following the pamphlet, I engaged in a system of alternating procedures. What seemed to work the best was two negative approaches – i.e., ignore SP after two incorrect incidents – followed by one positive approach – i.e., suggest Dairy Queen – and while I didn't see any immediate lessening of my father's drive to make what I thought of as mistakes, at least I was gaining some semblance of control over SP. At least that's what I wrote in my experiment journal: *Some semblance of control has been noted.*

o o o

Saturday morning at the breakfast table I initiated one distraction technique, trying to get my father to play catch with me by telling him that I was thinking of going out for a summer league baseball team – which, believe me, was miles from my mind. He agreed and we got our mitts and went to the park where we tossed the ball for an hour or so under Carol's watchful gaze.

Then, when we took a break, I could see him getting that look in his eye that always meant an afternoon of garage-sale trolling.

So I improvised and I suggested we take a trip to our town's nature centre, which my father liked almost as much as Dairy Queen. And where, coincidentally, it was impossible for him to buy or barter for anything that would embarrass me or nearly ruin my life as long as I kept him away from the gift shop or snack bar at the visitors centre.

An added benefit is that Carol could come with us, as long as we kept her on a leash. After burning a few hours of Carol pulling us along paths through meadows and woods looking at trees and shrubs and flowers and keeping her well clear of the duck pond to avoid stimulating her killing instincts, we got back in the truck. I thought it might be time to head home and put our feet up for the rest of the day when I noticed Carol start to look hard into my right eye with her upper lips quivering above those sparkling, shredding teeth.

So I asked SP to take us to the Dairy Queen. Carol relaxed, SP enjoyed himself, and another fashion disaster for yours truly, involving clothing or straw hats or flirty bottom dungarees, was averted.

When I reported to him later, Pooder said it wasn't me training them as much as it was Carol training me, and I suppose it could be viewed that way. You could say she was training me to take her to Dairy Queen every time I had worked on two negative attempts to correct my father's behaviour. You know. If you looked at it that way. Which I totally do. I mean, it was a dog-training manual, and Carol was a dog. She got it quicker than SP.

This was right about the time Pooder decided to become a professional golfer.

Thing is, he'd never played golf. Didn't know much about it. But his father had been flopped on the sofa sipping evening wine watching a golf tournament, and Pooder locked in on the game. And the potential riches that came from mastering the sport.

'Think about it,' he said. 'You hit a little white ball into a hole in the ground, and once you can do it better than other people, you make a ton of coin. How hard can it be?'

'It's maybe not that easy,' I pointed out. 'I read that an accurate definition of golf is a good walk ruined. They say it's so frustrating at times that many people have had heart attacks from the stress.'

'Because they weren't prepared. You just have to get some clubs and whack the ball around for a while until you get good at it and there you go – more coin than you know how to use.'

'But you don't have clubs. Do you even own a golf ball?'

Pooder snorted. 'Mere logistics. I again call your attention to the nearly completely successful frog-altitude experiment.' He lowered his eyes and covered his heart at the memory of how not entirely successful the frog-altitude experiment had been. 'Compared to the complications and danger of the frog-altitude experiment, how difficult can it be to procure some clubs and a ball and excel at hitting one with the other?'

And so Pooder worked on golf at the same time I continued working on varying my training procedures with SP and Carol.

There was, I realized when I reviewed my notes, no real lasting effect despite the abundance of ice cream cones. SP, for instance, bought what he called 'a whole wrapped brick' of boys' size small underwear briefs – 'they'll stretch out and if we're careful not to shrink them in hot water you'll have underwear until you're an old man' – during this time. He also bought a heavy-duty, commercial power belt sander that intermittently, independently, turned itself on. We didn't know that's why it had been on sale for so cheap until it suddenly roared to life, jumping away from a board and screaming after Carol, who had been napping in the shed and was explosively surprised. The sander flopped and bounced, and Carol barked, and it seemed to chase her until it hit the end of the cord and lost power, whereupon she turned and destroyed it. Like a skunk after chickens.

It was about then – when I was still thinking about how to make some actual money for the bike fund – that Pooder talked me into caddying at the local public golf course. 'Guys will pay you to carry their clubs around and you can get big tips. Make some good coin.'

Which wasn't true at the beginning. The golfers didn't give big tips. Mostly they screamed at their clubs and the weather and the golf balls and the hills and slopes that ruined par and the sun in their eyes and shade that made them misread distance and and and . . . The game should be called Tiny White Frustration Ball with Fairway and Tee.

Interestingly, about halfway around the nine-hole course, the players had to shoot across a small pond near the tee, and almost none of the golfers seemed to be able to avoid hitting the pond.

They'd line up their swing and you'd hear the club hit the ball with a loud *thwack!* followed seconds later by the quieter sound of the ball plunking into the pond.

'I'll bet,' Pooder said, eyeing the pond during a break as we drank water from a hose that watered the green, 'that the bottom of that pond is covered with golf balls. Enough balls are sitting in that pond that I'd never have to buy a ball the whole rest of my professional golfing career.'

And so, later that night, we took a burlap sack and rode our bikes to the golf course and salvage-dived in the pond for balls. The bottom was thick mud, but by feeling down a bit with our bare feet, we found the half-buried golf balls and then we'd flop over and dive down – it was only five feet or so deep – and push our hands in the muck and grab for anything firm and round. After a few hours and who knows how much mud we pawed through, we had found just under three hundred golf balls.

Two hundred and ninety-six exactly, Pooder wants me to say.

Pooder, as well as being inventive and

imaginative, is almost pure hustler. He figured that he'd only need, at most, four, better make it five just in case, golf balls to launch his career as a professional golfer, and so he hustled the club's golf pro, who ran the practice driving range, to buy the extra two hundred and ninety-one balls off him for twenty cents apiece.

Fifty-eight dollars and twenty cents.

Even split in half it gave us each twenty-nine dollars and ten cents of pure profit.

In the form of real money. Not just stored energy in the form of services to exchange and/ or barter for goods. And I thought – mistakenly, as it turned out – that I could use the fact that I earned extra money, real money, and not just energy-equivalent stuff to help convince my dad that it might be a good thing for him to do as well.

I brought what I thought to be the convincing information, i.e., the cold, hard cash, to my father's attention.

Major oops.

'What you've got there,' he told me, 'is probably

enough that, with thoughtful spending at garage sales and the second-hand clothes shop, might get you all your school clothes for the year if, you know, you shop carefully and, of course, not counting shoes and underwear, which you already have.'

Pooder, for once, agreed with me rather than siding with my dad. 'Twenty-nine dollars and ten cents won't get you a single decent T-shirt online, let alone at a shop. You know, where they have to charge more because they have overhead to think about . . .' He was beginning to lean away from golf, as autumn was coming, moving toward what he called 'a solid career' as an economist.

And, of course, he was right and my dad hadn't seen the appeal of cash in hand and the whole business sent me back to the drawing board, as they say, or, in reality, back to the pamphlet.

But first, my father accidentally tried to kill me.

THE HARLEY

I think it's important to understand at this time in our story that, along with my attempting to reboot my dad, other parts of our life went on.

We ate breakfast and dinner, slept each night in our beds in the trailer, fed varying numbers of chickens and the two pigs, scraped up and bucketed parts of shredded skunks that Carol caught and killed, fished and gardened – just kept on just living.

For my father, part of that just-living thing was the continual hunt for what he called bargains, not at garage sales, but in the shopper news circulars that came to our mailbox every Wednesday and Friday. When he found what he considered to be a particularly good item, he would approach the owners and begin – Pooder's definition now – the 'attack of Barterman'.

My father loved to barter. To trade, as he thought of it, energies, abilities, knowledge. Trade everything he could so as not use money. 'I have a widget,' he explained to me when I was very small, 'and John Doe has an extra electric frying pan he doesn't need, but he needs a widget and so we trade. We barter. Simple and clean. It's the very best and purest way to do business.'

'What's a widget?' Pooder asked when I was complaining again about how my dad spent energy and not money. 'Sounds like a smelly nocturnal animal.'

'A small mechanical device of no known origin,' I said. 'I looked it up on the internet and that's the informal definition. It's also a part of interfacing computers, but no one seems to be able to clearly explain how it fits in there, so I went with the informal usage. The word is sometimes misused when *gadget* would be more appropriate, as in—'

'Thank you.' Pooder, who has made tangents an art form, cut me off. 'So your dad likes to barter.'

'I think it's his breath of life. He loves the very idea of it.'

'But,' Pooder said. Full sentence.

'Exactly. Most people don't want to barter for things that are new and, well, the practice isn't exactly universally accepted. Plus, he's got involved with some strange trades because he wasn't careful and got caught up in the spirit of the thing rather than keeping his eye on endgame. I mean, not all the barters were failures or mistakes. He found a good rear-tine Troy-Bilt garden tiller that only needed some work on the motor and it makes gardening a snap. Way better than a hoe or pick and shovel, and he got it for a clothes dryer he had reconditioned with a new belt system.'

'So when it works,' Pooder said, 'it works. Bartering, I mean. But when it goes wrong, it can be a calamity.'

Like the Harley-Davidson.

I'm speaking, of course, of the Softail Harley

that Dad received in exchange for building a small stock barn for goats and chickens from an ex-biker named CB.

I had asked my dad what the initials stood for, and he said it was short for his nickname, which was Coffinbreath. While it was true CB's breath didn't smell like a blast of mint, it wasn't that bad (not like, say, standing downwind of Oscar or sleeping with Carol in the summer after she'd killed a skunk), and even though it didn't feel wise to ask CB how he got the nickname, I was still curious.

When I mentioned the mystery to Pooder, he said I was smart to let it go. 'It's never wrong to act with restraint of pen and tongue. Especially when it's an ex-biker whose nickname is Coffinbreath. You might wind up as a bonnet ornament.'

But CB was nice enough and said they needed the building because he and 'his woman' were going to be farmers. CB's woman had a name, Priddy, but you wouldn't know listening to him talk about her because I mainly heard him call her 'my woman'. As in, 'My woman needs a place for her animals now that we're going to raise our own livestock and live green and all that crap.' Or, 'My woman wants me to milk goats so I'll need a stand for them because my back and knees and all that crap are shot from all the years on the bike.' And, 'My woman says I can learn to milk goats and all that crap even though I keep telling her I'm better with engines than teats.'

CB may have talked like a sexist pig but it was clear he did pretty much anything 'his woman' asked.

My dad was happy with the proposed exchange. 'Getting a Harley is perfect for future bartering. Everybody wants a Harley,' he said, as we watched CB roll the bike (what CB called 'a hog' and what Priddy called 'the loud, two-wheeled, like, death machine that I've, you know, had enough of already, damn') out of their garage to show us what a great deal my dad was making. ('They're always in, like, great demand,' Priddy added. Maybe she was worried my dad was thinking of backing out, which he wasn't.)

When I told Pooder about the Harley, he nearly drooled. 'Chicks dig Harleys,' he said. 'We can ride around and they'll flock to us.'

I thought that sort of language didn't sound right coming from a budding economist, and so I looked at him and said, 'Chicks?' in the same tone as I would say 'Homework over the summer holidays?'

He rolled his eyes and said, 'Get a grip, man, we're of an age to think that way.'

There are times when you correct your friend for being an archaic sexist pig like CB and then there are times when you sit back and wait for karma to drop-kick his disrespectful butt into gentlemanly manners. I chose the latter because who am I to deprive some budding feminist of the chance to put Pooder in his place? Sometimes you learn more from painful example than helpful warning. And I already had my hands full trying to train my dad.

So my father built a small shed and a goat barn for Priddy and CB and naturally I helped, and for a time there, life wasn't bad. The work kept us from going to garage sales or second-hand clothes shops, and for a couple of weeks, I didn't even have to worry about positive or negative reinforcement techniques.

Carol came with us to CB and Priddy's place, of course, and quickly developed a bond with CB – they seemed to speak the same language, which was essentially a series of grumbles and grunts – and it kept her from staring into my right eye.

Plus, I made a new friend. One afternoon when we were working on the roof and I was running back and forth handing shingles up to Dad (I should mention that I was wearing a set of the pale-pink dungarees with the faded word JUICY written across the butt), Priddy came up to me.

'Love your dungarees,' she said. 'I have, like, the exact same pair. You can come over after we, like, get a goat, anytime you want and have fresh goat milk. Like, on the house. After, you know, CB learns to, like, milk a goat.'

I nodded and smiled and thanked her even though I was fairly certain I wouldn't think much of the taste of goat milk, much less go out of my way to get a free cup. I didn't think CB was, like, you know, going to start milking goats soon. (Turns out I was wrong on both counts: CB did learn to milk a goat, which he named Betty, and I wound up, like, enjoying fresh goat milk.)

So there finally came a morning when CB rode up our dirt driveway on the motorcycle with mufflers that sounded like machine guns, and parked it in front of our trailer; then Priddy drove him home in her Prius. I thought I saw a tear in CB's eyes when he walked away from the bike, but it could have been my imagination. I don't think he cried often.

And suddenly we had a Harley-Davidson motorcycle.

There it sat, about four feet from our mailbox at the side of the path leading up to the porch. I hadn't thought much about it until there it was, in our garden, shining in the sun, visible from every window on one side of the trailer.

A Harley-Davidson motorcycle, for those of you who don't know, is nothing short of magic.

Dazzling. Mesmerizing. Captivating.

The closer you get and the longer you're near one, the stronger its hold on you.

All right, I know not everybody gets all side-wiggled at the sight of a motorcycle. But put yourself in my shoes and think, having never ridden anything without pedals, having never gone anywhere except in a beat-up old Chevy pickup that made enough rattling sounds to make you think earplugs were as essential to travel as seat belts, think what the motorcycle meant to me.

There is, simply, nothing on earth cooler than a Harley-Davidson. And, if you own one, which we miraculously did, you simply called it a 'Harley'.

It was like America – all the best parts of a wonderful, pure, American Dream America – had suddenly moved into our garden, covered in chrome and shining bright silver in the sun. Everything in me, every cell, wanted me to go out and get on that Harley – *the* Harley – and fire it up and thunder down the road into the rest of my life forever and ever, amen.

After I stopped and asked Peggy if she wanted to go for a ride on something majestic and manly and then the wind would blow her hair around and her eyes would laugh and she'd sit in back of me and hold on tight around my waist . . .

Pooder says I'm getting off topic again, but he understands the intoxicating effect of the bike and thinks you will, too, so we're leaving it in.

Although I couldn't drive yet, I did go out and sit on the Harley and balanced it enough to knock up the kickstand and sort of semi-pretend I was riding it, cranking the handgrip throttle and making motor sounds in my mind. But Harleys are very heavy and I started to lean and then lean more and suddenly I was about to lose control and I was covered in sweat and my arms and legs were shaking as I tried to right the bike before it tipped over on me. I barely got it balanced and back upright again so I could put the kickstand down, which was nothing short of a full and complete miracle because Harley-Davidsons weigh between five hundred and forty and nine hundred and five pounds, and I only weighed about a hundred and five, and being smushed by a Harley in your own front garden is the second worst way to be taken out by one after losing control on the freeway and sliding under a semi and . . .

Carol stood by and watched the whole thing and was, I think, concerned that, first, I had somehow stolen the bike from her new best friend, CB, and second, I had gone completely insane. But she was a lot less displeased than when I'd tried to distract her and SP from garage sales so she didn't show me her teeth or stare at my right eye.

My father had propped up the Harley and wandered off to do other things in his shed. I thought he'd forgotten about it, and to be frank, I'd been so caught up in dreams of the Harley that he could have disappeared altogether for all I'd noticed. Harleys have a blinding effect.

I mean, he had been there all along, of course, and once I noticed him again, I could tell he was getting ready to return to his normal way of living, and by that I mean hitting garage sales, and I was on the edge of firing up the reinforcement program again. But I didn't have to, because the Harley saved me.

Well, at least at first.

Because there came a morning when he was sitting in the kitchen drinking coffee, looking out the window while I had some porridge, and staring at the Harley, and his eyes looked a little different. Had a warm shine in them, a glint, and he said softly, 'CB said there were some problems with the fuel system. Maybe I should check it out.'

And I thought, oh no. Not the fuel system.

He had some mystical knowledge about fuel systems in engines. He knew things – Dark, Secret Basement Things – about fuel systems and their potential. He would take the most ordinary tools such as a spanner and a screwdriver and a magnifying glass and set in to tinkering, and the engine would become altered. That's the way to put it, too – *altered* – he would take it to an altered state, no longer a normal, sensible, peace-loving engine, but a fuel-devouring, insanely powerful, roaring monster.

My dad's particular talent vis-à-vis fuel systems had led to such disasters as the famous Wood Chipper Horror, where he bartered his labour working on an engine-driven wood chipper for a stack of roof shingles. My dad 'tuned' the fuel system on the motor, and according to the new owner when he fired it up, the chipper went berserk and reversed course, spewing instead of chipping, and driving the three-foot two-by-four completely through the front and back of his new car, smashing the front windshield and rear window to smithereens, and he swore, 'taking Binky right out' when he hit the stop button and the chipper seemed to take a deep breath, then inhale everything. Simply everything not nailed down.

Binky was the pet cat of the guy's wife, who claimed Binky got tangled in the seething vortex of swirling debris in the chipper's swath of destruction and was eaten whole and obliterated.

That's how she put it in a complaint letter from the lawyer: 'The chipper ate my whole cat.'

Which, if you think about it, is better than if the

chipper had only partially eaten her cat and all you had is, well, leftover cat. Personally, I think Binky just ran off as soon as the chipper fired up, heading for sanctuary where there was no Frankenstein wood chipper, because cats are smart and fast.

In any case, Binky was permanently missing, so we got the lady a new kitten from Oscar's yard and her husband promised her that he would never run the wood chipper if the new whole cat was outside. My dad and I helped him drag the chipper to an open field behind his house where it couldn't suck up debris and produce another hurricane-force blast. The lawyer who sent the letter saying he looked forward to taking Dad to court and winning 'substantial damages for emotional suffering and property damage' took one look at our 1951 half-ton dented Chevy pickup and me in my pink dungarees, threw up his hands, muttering something about lost causes, and then kicked us out of his office. Dad smiled and told me that mitigation is far superior to litigation in terms of legal problem solving.

But imagine my horror when my father took his toolbox and started on the Harley's fuel system. I can't count on baby cats to fix all the problems my dad causes with his fuel-system tinkering.

'Isn't that sacrilege?' Pooder said when I told him my dad was working on the Harley.

'Sacrilege?' I said, wondering where he found that word and whether he was now wanting to become a pastor or some spiritual leader because I didn't think I could handle a Pooder who went around testifying and singing uplifting songs and badgering me to confess my sins so I could walk free in the light of forgiveness.

'Yeah. You know. For him to work on a Harley like that. Aren't they already, well, perfect? And if you mess with them, aren't you committing a form of sacrilege? A violation of concept?'

'It's what he does,' I said, shrugging and thinking I'd have to find out what Pooder was reading because he was using a lot of new big words and seemed to know what they meant, and I wanted to rule out the worry that he'd found religion. 'Since it doesn't interfere with my retraining concept, I'm going to leave well enough alone.' I threw my own use of the word *concept* in there so he didn't think I was completely ignorant.

Except, of course, I was totally ignorant of what was about to happen.

But sometimes ignorance is bliss, and so, for a brief, happy time, SP worked on the Harley fuel system and wasn't out doing things that ruined my life with embarrassment; life was pleasant, and Carol, who'd managed to annihilate a skunk and something that might have been a gopher – it was so hard to tell what the leftover bits had once been that I called her Wood Chipper for a few days – left my right eye alone.

But nothing good lasts forever, and so my happy time drew to a close. There came the moment when Dad finished working on the Harley and started the motor.

It had been loud when CB brought it over. Like a machine gun, as I said before. But now, with my father's Secret Knowledge Work on the fuel system, now . . .

The Harley produced a sound that seemed to come from inside my own body, my own soul. A deep, resonating, thudding roar like thunder right after a lightning bolt hits a tree nearby. A ground-shaking, pulse-changing explosion that went in my ears and rumbled around in each cell of my being and came out of every pore of my body.

A Harley turned loose.

My father was sitting on it. He saw me and yelled over the engine roar: 'GET YOUR HELMET AND COME FOR A RIDE!'

I think that's what he said. I was reading his lips because there was no sound but the Harley. And I've got to be honest, for just a beat, I thought of refusing him because I was a little afraid of getting on what now seemed like a wild beast.

But the part of me that had apparently been created without self-preservation instincts, which was proof positive I was my father's son and Pooder's best friend, took over and thought, if I didn't get on the bike, if I didn't do this one thing, and I eventually became an old man, would I not wonder all my days what it would have been like if I *had* got on the bike?

And so, I got my helmet, which was an old football helmet from a garage sale that had BRONCOS stamped on the side of it, clamped it on my head, and straddled the bike on what I learned later was called the sissy seat. Wearing pink dungarees and a football helmet, I recklessly yelled into my father's ear: 'Let's go!'

It turns out I was not ready for anything that happened next, which was all right because I don't have a good, clear memory of the next three and a half minutes.

Which, coincidentally, was the precise length of the ride.

I remember looking down and back as my dad cranked the hand-throttle and gave the bike gas. I could see jets of flame a foot long blow out the rear of the exhaust system, and I thought, *Wow*. Just that. *Wow. Fire.*

I didn't think Harleys were supposed to shoot fire out the rear like that.

The motorcycle leaped forward, roaring as the

tyres caught the gravel driveway and screeched down the length of it – approximately a hundred and fifty yards – where the drive curved away from the river and cut into the main road.

I don't know how fast we were going as we neared the end of the drive and approached the upcoming bend, but I vaguely remember realizing there was no way we were going to make the curve.

I felt my father's body stiffen in terror-shock-fright at the sudden raw power and drastic acceleration of the motorcycle and I knew in an instant that his control of the bike and ability as a driver were nowhere near enough to combat the speed and power of the bike as we hurtled toward a turn we couldn't possibly handle.

The bike powered straight ahead, thundering through time and space, soaring off the end of the drive, propelled into the air, clearing the riverbank neatly – as if my father had planned it – in a perfect parabolic curve, before crash-landing with a giant splash in the middle of the river – both still sitting on the seat, Dad clutching the handlebars, me clutching Dad.

As might be reasonably imagined, the bike did not float. (Pooder wants me to remind you that I already told you that Harleys weigh between five hundred and forty and nine hundred and five pounds.)

The plunge paralyzed us – half surprise and panic, half shock and horror – and we were sucked down, some fifteen feet or so, to the riverbed by the weight of the motorcycle.

Before I could kick loose, I'm pretty sure I swallowed close to a gallon of muddy river water and mother earth only knows how much turtle poop.

But in seconds (which felt like days as my life flashed before my eyes), our survival mode kicked in and we broke free of the sinking Harley's suction and struggled to the surface, before clawing our way back to the muddy riverbank where we dragged our way out of the water and lay sputtering and gasping in the thick grunge.

My father, gagging on muck, rasped: 'You know, I don't think I did that exactly right.'

GUN, SQUIRT, ONE EACH

Turns out we weren't motorcycle people.

Dad borrowed a wrecker with a massive hydraulic lifting arm – it shows the strength of his bartering system that he could 'borrow' a wrecker – and after many fruitless attempts, we finally snagged the bike with a grappling hook and dragged it out of the mud and lifted it out of the river.

Because the motor had been running hot when it hit the cold river water, the engine block cracked. Then, too, hooking and snagging and clawing at it with a grappling hook until it came loose from the mud didn't help the frame and suspension much, and by the time we got it out of the water and back in our garden, the Harley – the beautiful, perfect, powerful Harley – was totalled.

'It's like modern art,' Pooder said, trying to find something positive. 'Like somebody's make-believe sculpture of what a motorcycle should look like. You know, if you threw one at King Kong and he squished it in a massive hand. Makes good experimental lawn art. You could put it out front there and plant some flowers in it and people would think you meant it to be a unique garden feature. Good conversation starter. Just keep adding new pieces to it from time to time – say, you get what's left of that football helmet bronzed and put it on top – and when I finally get some fame going and people are so interested in me that they want to know all about my best friend, too, you could charge people to see it. Pick up some good coin . . .'

My father, however, didn't want to have anything more to do with the motorcycle.

Usually an outcome like this would inspire him to get back to work, repair it, make it better, retrace his steps, and work out the bugs, but not this time.

He was done with the Harley, and he used the

wrecker to lift it up and put it in the back of the truck, which we then drove to Old Oscar's. Where he dumped it and left it. Done and gone.

But even out of sight and out of mind, the Harley seemed to have a lasting influence on Dad. And not for the better.

I think he viewed it as a failure, and to make up for his disappointment in his own skills, he apparently mentally resolved to rack up as many successes as he could.

He (and by he, I mean Dad, Carol, and I) absolutely attacked garage sales, and read and followed up on ads touting 'barter-for-goods' in the free local shopping flyers. I was so busy doing two negative reinforcements followed by one positive attempt that the whole time became a bewildering blur and I hardly had the energy at night to log my attempts and their subsequent outcome in my notebook.

The puppy-food brochure assured me that persistence and patience were everything, so I stayed the course, as best I could.

But then something happened that was so

socially devastating that . . . well, you'll see. Pooder says this is what's called building suspense and that every good book should have some.

It was getting towards the end of summer, and the supermarket in town was bursting with new produce. Which meant the dumpster behind the supermarket where we got food to feed the pigs seemed to almost explode with battered and wilting vegetables and bruised fruit and all kinds of other surplus potential pig food like marble rye bread and expired tubs of yogurt and freezer-burned frozen pizzas.

On one trip, as we pulled around and parked the truck behind the supermarket, we found a hog gold mine. There were thirty pounds of containers of whipping cream, close to forty packages of slightly spoiled strawberries, and eleven outdated angel food cakes.

It was a full load by itself and we hurried to get it in the truck and then rush back to the pigs. We ripped open the containers of whipping cream and poured them in the trough, dumped in the strawberries and stacked the cakes on top. The effect was immediate. The pigs literally submerged their heads in the cream, hunting berries, raising at intervals to get a breath and slurp down a large chunk of cake before ducking back under, snort-snuffling and bubbling and chewing in ecstasy.

There's nothing as joyful as a feeding pig. You can take my word on that one.

We were dumping the last batch of treats, hurrying so we could get back to the supermarket for another load of dumpster goodies, when I stepped wrong, tripped, stumbled, and fell headfirst toward the trough full of cream. As I was falling, I tucked and rolled, twisting away from the trough, so I landed on the mucky ground.

I hoped what I fell in was mud, but I am not that lucky and the smell quickly indicated that it was way more than wet dirt. As Pooder tells me several times every day he comes over to our place, there is very little on the planet that stinks worse than pig poop.

Since we were aiming to make another run back to the supermarket to get a load of vegetables before they were taken away by the rubbish truck, my dad said I didn't have time to shower and change clothes. 'Just do a quick rinse with the hose at the side of the pigpen, give yourself a good shake, and with the windows of the truck wide-open, you'll be air-dried by the time we get to town.'

I was, of course, wearing a pair of pink dungarees and the pig poop didn't 'hose off' like magic, and I started to kick up a fuss about changing because I didn't want to wear pig-poop-saturated pink dungarees into town, even to go dumpster diving, but Dad was freaking out about losing our 'window of opportunity'.

'We don't want miss a whole load of good veggies,' he said. 'Pigs can't live by cake and cream alone – we have to balance their diet. Nobody will see you. It'll be fine.'

I had, over the last week, worked in the garden without a hat, and my nose and the tops of my ears were badly sunburned, which gave me a purple-nosed, flopping-red-ears disaster fashion look, and to cap it off – no pun intended – I was wearing the big straw hat.

With the see-through green visor in the front.

And because Dad drove the truck, which had no air conditioning, with windows open and a fast wind blew through the side from the little butterfly windows at the front of the door-windows, I had needed to quickly retie the chin strap to hold it on my head because the frayed piece of orange-coloured baler twine kept breaking.

Pink-dungareed, poop-covered, straw-hatted, red-eared-and-nosed – your basic complete clown costume – headed for the dumpster riding shotgun in a beat-up, more-than-half-a-century-old truck next to a pit bull that kept smiling at me while she studied my right eye.

Totally cool.

But my dad was probably right – nobody would see me.

This is probably a good time to introduce a new character to the story we're putting together here. Her name is Marge. She is an elderly woman who roams around town and the nearby countryside calling herself the 'Video Reporter'. That means that she went looking for interesting things to record with her phone and then edited stories – hard-hitting news packages, if you will – before pitching them to the local news station. Most of her stuff never saw the light of the television studios, but . . .

You already know where this is going, don't you.

I noticed her truck in the car park in front of the supermarket – an older Toyota with flowers and strange lightning bolts painted on the side – and, if I thought about her at all, I assumed she was shopping for groceries.

But no.

Without our knowledge or consent or permission or approval or legal waiver, she took several videos of us, apparently shooting from around the corner of the supermarket, and sent them into the news channel with a colour commentary voice-over:

'Showing how to live in a completely green, sustainable manner, a local family gathers unwanted food to feed themselves and livestock. A father-and-son duo prove it can be done.'

And there I was, in all my glory, rooting around in the dumpster, featured as the human interest slot of the evening news.

At five o'clock, six o'clock, and, in case you missed it, again at eleven. And, because that's how these things go, all over the TV station's multiple social media platforms as well.

In living colour.

Let me repeat the image in case it's faded from your mind.

Red nose, folded-over red-tipped ears, mud-and-poop-covered pink dungarees, and a straw hat held down by a tightly tied, frayed orange piece of baler twine, grabbing armloads of what can only be called sloppy rubbish out of a dumpster accompanied by a pit bull who did notice that she was being filmed and was, I swear, giving her best and brightest smile for the camera.

Look, I *know* it's not completely my father's fault. He didn't know that the sniper-reporter would catch sight of us and see the newsworthy aspect of our endeavours; it's not the type of thing, I admit, that anyone could predict and then avoid.

But all of this is, in a very real way, directly due to his actions and philosophy about not using money because that's where the ridiculous clothes I had to wear came from. Pooder pointed out that I ended that sentence with a preposition and I should have mentioned that the clothes were beside the point and that the dumpster diving was the primary source of humiliation for me.

So it was not entirely, but mostly, my dad's fault. Even so, I was the one who got inundated by the storm of emails, subject line 'Bin Boy' and 'Waste Warrior' and 'Rubbish Guy,' because my dad doesn't even have email, does he?

My father's only comment when he saw the news clip and the social media posts and the emails: 'Good coverage, accurate take on our quality example of sustainable living. We are so ahead of the curve on this one. Just watch, we probably kicked off a new trend.'

'Excellent pictures,' Pooder said the morning

after what he called the news breakout. 'Marge must have done some updating on her video app. I could easily tell it was you. Heck, it even shows your eye colour and some of the lower cheek pimples.'

Oh good, I thought. Pimples. Why not? I mean, I understand it's not like I started on a very high social plane, but this did it: I was socially ruined. As in, was it possible for me to move alone to another country and get a new name? That kind of ruined.

'It could be worse,' Pooder said.

'How?'

He opened his mouth to explain, instantly realized he couldn't, and immediately changed course. 'Here's how you handle this: Just own it. Put out a statement that you were having a bad-clothes day because what's the point of wearing nice clothes when you dumpster dive for pig food, and then people won't think you're completely fashion-handicapped. Problem handled.'

Put out a statement. Right. Then I did something I've never done before – I walked away from Pooder before he could figure out a way to make this debacle part of his future plans to make some good coin.

And so.

Back to the pamphlet.

Which said – not quoting, but another paraphrase here – that if the subtle negative approach to positive reinforcement didn't prove successful, it might be wise to go to a more physical negative concept.

They said to try a squirt gun with water.

And do it hidden somehow so that if the SP started to do something incorrect, say mess on the floor, just squirt him, or her, with water when SP wasn't looking. So the SP will simply be confused and bewildered by the sudden drops of water seemingly out of nowhere and his attention will be distracted momentarily so you can run something positive into the situation in that moment.

Which sounds pretty uncomplicated except that the pamphlet writer wasn't constantly being observed by a pit bull named Carol, who was already suspicious of me and probably certain I had somehow wrecked the Harley that she seemed to think was on loan from CB, whom she loved.

And it turns out she had a thing about guns. Which I did not know at the time, but will now never forget.

I bought a package of small plastic toy squirt guns, so tiny that one of them would almost totally fit in my hand and pocket and they were in fact pink – which was good because I didn't want anybody to mistake them for a real gun that I might be seen aiming at my father now that I was a talking point around town. I filled one with water at the kitchen sink when Dad was outside, and started to put it in my back pocket.

Carol had been in the trailer with me, studying me closely, and as I moved away from the sink and turned to put the mini pink squirt gun in my pocket, she jumped up, grabbed the gun neatly – almost surgically – from my hand, and, levering her vice-like jaws (and we've already talked about pressure per square inch in terms of her bite if you'll recall how she eats Dairy Queen vanilla ice cream cones), made it into a not-squirt gun. What she made it into was, in fact, a handful of little wet pink plastic splinters.

She looked a little bewildered at first, at the

spray-splash of water, then she spit-shook the wreckage onto the floor, and smiled at me, peering intently into my right eye.

All right, I thought, she didn't like that one.

She growled at me. Sound like distant thunder. Sound like maybe I was going to die here. Sound werewolves make when they're ready to attack. Sound you might hear as you're circling the drain . . .

But I steeled myself, took out another squirt gun, turned back toward the sink to start to fill it. This time, she jumped up, snatched it out of my hand before I could start filling it with water, and crushed it.

There had been four squirt guns in the plastic wrapper bag, and she systematically destroyed all four of them, and then grabbed the empty bag from my hand and ripped it to pieces like it was a skunk that had grated on her last nerve.

So she didn't like squirt guns, I thought, relieved that I still had both hands. I chewed on that for a bit while I dried the floor and swept up the plastic shards.

Carol had come from a hard place Back When – before we found her and brought her home and she started shoplifting at garage sales when she wasn't eating ice cream cones and killing skunks – and perhaps there were some bad memories of firearms in her mind.

In deference to her past trauma, because even though she smiles at me scary-like and tries to stop me from training SP, I have a lot of respect for her resilience and I appreciate that she's still loving and sweet despite her bad start in life (which is more than I can say for a lot of people). I realized I would have to figure out a different way to squirt water because I thought I was onto something with this strategy; the pamphlet raved about the efficacy of squirting water as a training tool.

So I bought a small squirt bottle – they were sold as plant misters, but the nozzle could be adjusted from mist to stream and they'd get the job done – at the DIY shop.

Which Carol didn't seem to mind.

And which worked perfectly.

And which I started to use right after my father accidentally tried to kill Pooder.

DEATH BY WATER SKI

So far this chronicle here has primarily been about my father's philosophies and the effect they had on me. The negative effect they had on me. The *really* negative effect they had on me. So negative I thought they might be ruining my life.

Like that level of negativity.

But Pooder has been reading along as I transcribe this, even proofreading at certain places and offering some solid editorial advice, like how I should add undercarriage to the story and make sure the catalyst is clear, and I love him for that even though it's not my style, but I know he wants the best for me and my book – and he downloaded a grammar book to have on hand so that he could tell me the difference between a predicate and a diphthong and other writing technical stuff like that.

o o o

Sorry for the break here, but we had to look up *diphthong*. Lots of definitions, but the simplest one is that it's a sliding vowel. Which still doesn't make a lot of sense but now Pooder says I have to tell the joke that went around when we were in the fourth grade: What do you get if you shake a can of alphabet soup? A vowel movement . . . Not great, I admit, you'd be in stitches if you were nine years old. (Pooder's still laughing.)

So anyway, Pooder has been reading and proofing this all along and has decided he should – how did he put it? – oh yeah, he wants to be more evident in the story.

I pointed out to him that this history wasn't really about him. I was the one wearing the pink dungarees and straw hat held down with baler twine playing around in a dumpster full of trash and splashed – and that's a good word for it – splashed across the television screen for all the world to see, and in the final analysis, it wasn't his father, but mine. Then I ran a word search and found that we had plenty of *Pooder* already in the book – one hundred and thirty so far, to be exact.

'Still,' he countered – and since he had recently decided again to be a famous lawyer he could, actually, counter – holding one finger up. 'I have read this as you go and offered good criticism that kept you from making big mistakes, so I think it's natural and fair for me to be in there more often.'

And because he's a good friend and persuasive and – when it's all said and done – he had a lot to add that was helpful at the very end, and he is the next part of this story anyway, here goes.

But first, a few quick descriptive notes, thoughts, and actions of, on, and by Pooder:

The most important thing to consider about him is that, although he can seem ridiculous and off-the-wall when he's working at his crazy and far-fetched what-he's-becoming phases, they are real to him.

Pooder has the admirable if mind-boggling and sometimes annoying and almost always confusing ability to live in his dreams to the extent that he knows, absolutely *knows*, they could come true; he firmly and totally believes with every fibre of his being and every last cell of his body that he could become that Viking or fighter pilot or lawyer or judge, not only become, but eventually be *the best* Viking or pilot or lawyer or judge ever. Or linguistics professor, English teacher, Brit-forensic-scientist-slash-detective . . . you get the picture.

I hate to admit that he's really amazing.

But.

And there's always a 'but' just as there's always a 'thing'.

But.

The but is that he drags this sureness, this imaginary potential ability, into everything that comes along.

He thinks he becomes an expert at anything he sets his mind to even if it's something he's never done before, and this has led to some complications and difficulties in his and my life. Because he is so persuasive, it's easy to get swept up in his actions, especially when he thinks I need to take my mind off my troubles, and by 'my troubles', I mean my dad.

Plus, he said, summer was coming to an end and he had some bucket-list items he hadn't checked off yet that he needed to get done before we went back to school. It was only fair. The whole rest of the summer he had listened to me chew on the problem of training my dad; he deserved a good wingman for a couple weeks.

I didn't think he'd take it that literally.

He dragged me off to Murchinson's Hill, an elevation south of town that's high enough to draw people who want to use their hang gliders for relatively short trips.

It was cool to watch them, and I thought we were going to sit on the hill and make bets on how long everyone stayed up and how far they went, but Pooder got that look in his eye, and before I knew what happened, he had convinced one of the hang gliders (shockingly easily, if you ask me;

I would have guessed it would have been tougher to sweet-talk your way into a death-defying leisure time activity that is surely riddled with insurance policies and indemnity clauses) that he, Pooder, was nearly an expert at hang gliding and wouldn't it be okay, glider guy to glider guy, if he 'took a short hop'.

That's how Pooder put it — a short hop.

Well.

It wasn't a hop and it wasn't short.

They strapped him in and he trundled off down the hill like a more or less ruptured duck, wobbling under the weight of that hang glider. The helmet he borrowed was too large and it slipped down and twisted around his head until it was blocking his forward and peripheral vision.

I guess I should have been worried about his complete blindness, but since it was clearly obvious that he didn't know the first thing about hang gliding, I was convinced he wouldn't get airborne at all. I figured I'd be picking him out of a faceplant in the grass in another twenty seconds or so.

But.

There was a 'wind snort', which is how Pooder put it later, ripping up the hill, and it snaked in under the wing and instantly, violently shot the glider and an attached-but-blinded Pooder up forty or fifty feet, exactly high enough, Pooder said, that he could feel the atmospheric pressure change and make his ears pop, like in an aeroplane, and he thought he might mess his pants.

That's not quite as graphic as he put it, but we'll go with that here.

He took off like a shot, away from the hill, hanging limply in the glider and, I thought, screaming, but he swears he wasn't, for nearly a mile to the edge of Happy Buckaroo Riding Stables – a charming little place where people brought small children to ride the ponies.

The wind held steady for a beat, and the glider, you know, glided, despite the fact that the alleged pilot didn't have a single clue what he was doing.

But gravity being what it is (an immutable fact of nature, Pooder wants me to say), he eventually came down. With the same surprising force that took him up in the first place.

He landed – plunged like a clay pigeon in an Olympic skeet-shooting event, to be accurate – in the centre of a small pasture where fifteen Shetland ponies were peacefully grazing.

Here's a note to file away for future reference: Shetland ponies are small, you might even go so far as to call them cute because they look like you could cuddle and hug them, but the truth is they can be as mean as junkyard dogs when startled, and all of them, from the first to the last in the history of the breed, have the famous Napoleon complex: *If you're small, fight. Right now. Just jump in the middle of it and kill it. No matter what it is.*

And all of them, led by a vicious little monster named Clyde, centred their startled, high-strung, purebred-pony rage on the multicoloured bird of prey that had crash-landed in their field.

They descended on Pooder and the glider like four-legged avenging Huns.

Pooder, still half blinded by the twisted helmet,

crawled – I thought a more apt word might be *slith-ered* – away from the herd of tiny but furious horses and under a fence where he collapsed and started breathing again.

'I am,' he said, gasping as I arrived (the other hang gliders had given me a lift from the take-off spot to the farm and even provided me with a pair of binoculars so I could track his flight pattern), 'suddenly very sympathetic with the frogs from the altitude experiment, even the ones from the non-lethal attempts, and frankly just glad to be alive.'

And while he/we never again talked of his short-lived but quickly aborted (we hightailed it out of there while the other hang gliders rescued the glider from the ponies) career as a hang-glider pilot, it remained as a good example of the trouble he could find even on a soft summer day with a breeze at the top of a gentle hill with the best of intentions and the heart of a Wright brother.

That he lived through this disaster at all is only a matter of luck – the Shetland ponies alone could have killed him – and that makes it doubly strange that in the end what nearly finished him was something he genuinely *did* know how to do, was an expert at doing.

Water-skiing.

Two things to note:

First, in spite of his father's discovery of the difference between day wine and night wine and all the sports channels on television and how comfortable the recliner could be after a long workday, Pooder's family had taken an annual summer holiday north in the lake country. The resort they went to had all sorts of summer activities, including water-skiing, and Pooder spent almost every day skiing around the lake behind a relatively fast speedboat being piloted by a bored resort worker while his parents lounged by the pool. The resort lived in terror of being sued so they warned the personnel not to do anything wild or risky, which meant they were only allowed to make large, slow circles on the lake with the water skier.

While it was very tame and safe, Pooder did a huge amount of water-skiing and became something of an expert – not doing jumps, except small ones over the boat wake, or spins or any out of control tricks – but he was a proficient and able skier.

The other thing to note is that my father had fixed up an old Ford F-150 and later swapped it for a fibreglass speedboat with what he called a 'significant' outboard motor and a trailer to haul it around in back of our pickup. As I previously mentioned, we live on the edge of a river – where the Harley came to disaster – and in front of our place, the water was about a quarter of a mile across. It wasn't too pretty – Pooder said it 'wasn't resorty' – and the shore was muddy, but it was still a good-size body of water and someone before us had put in a small dock in front of the property.

Dad slid the boat into the water and we had to hand-paddle it over to the dock with two canoe paddles that came with the boat because – and this is important, a strongly pivotal moment – the motor wouldn't start.

Didn't even fire. Just a click and then silence.

And as I headed for the trailer to dry off and

change and my dad headed for his workshop, I heard him mutter – more pivotable information that will make sense to you from earlier in the book – 'I think there's something wrong with the fuel system.'

Well, sure, I knew where this could go.

A minute later I watched him head back to the boat with his toolbox and a gleam in his eye that made me think immediately of the wood chipper and the Harley and his penchant for making fuel systems become something just short of nuclear-grade powerful.

But the boat was in the water, I thought.

And water is soft, I thought.

How could anything go seriously wrong when you're only dealing with something as soft as water?

Oops.

It turns out that any activity that involves coming into contact with water also involves the absolute science of velocity. At slow speeds, water is definitely soft and, in fact, could be called gentle and even inviting.

But at high speed, things change dramatically

and impact at even twenty or thirty miles an hour can give plain water some of the characteristics of hardened cement.

And as we have learned, anytime my father dives into a fuel system, it always ends with a serious increase in power.

Which usually equals a similar increase in velocity.

So it came to pass that a few hours later, when I returned from a ride on my recumbent, he pronounced the motor repaired and, as he put it, 'humming like a clock'.

I had been away from the dock area and had not heard the motor humming like a clock or anything else. But when my father said he'd fixed the enormous outboard, I immediately called Pooder, eager to finally see his skiing skills in person because I was sure his stories about his annual water-skiing exploits were highly exaggerated and – may all the creatures that dwell underwater forgive me – told him to bring his skis and a towrope for the first test run.

He arrived in bathing trunks on his bicycle,

wearing a ski vest, with the towrope over his shoulder and the skis tied with clothesline rope to the rear carrier rack.

'I'm ready,' he said. 'Let's get our ski on.'

He looked so happy, with the golden sun shining down on his light hair and that big smile. I must have been grinning, too.

My dad was beaming and even Carol was wiggling all over.

I like to think back sometimes to how confident we all were, how sure of ourselves, how dry and mud-free and safe and static on dry ground we all were.

Good times.

We tied the towrope to a cleat on the rear transom of the boat and coiled the rope for quick release. Pooder sat on the dock holding the crossbar handle at the end of the rope.

He insisted on the dock-start, which he said he'd done many times at the lake.

Carol and I sat in the stern of the boat looking back, and my father sat at the controls in the bow.

Then he started the motor.

I had never before listened carefully to the sound of an outboard motor, but I remembered later that, instead of the promised humming, the motor more or less snorted, a deep, thrumming sound that echoed off the water and sent vibrations through the boat. I could feel the vibrations deep in my chest.

When my dad nudged the control lever to the forward position, we chugged slowly away from the dock. I watched the towline gradually uncoil, and when it came nearly to the end, I called, 'All right!'

My father evenly increased the speed and everything started out textbook perfect. The rope grew taut and Pooder left the dock cleanly and was almost instantly standing on his skis and even gave a quick wave to show it was going well. I threw my arm around Carol and settled back in the seat.

Pooder had a beautiful dry start.

Flawless in every way.

Except.

The motor behaved perfectly at first, but as I said, it didn't sound very happy. It sort of coughed and snarled and even I could sense that it somehow wanted more than the gentle, controlled pace my dad kept, a moderate proper skiing speed.

A flicker of alarm passed through my brain. The motor seemed impatient and frustrated to be so reined in.

Near the centre of the river, with a sickening lurch and a ferocious roar that made my bones vibrate, the motor went ahead and broke free, going full throttle.

We found later that Dad had decided that the systems governing fuel delivery to the firing chambers in the motor was in some way restricted, and that's why it hadn't been running when he took delivery.

But being the mechanical wizard he is, my father 'tweaked' the fuel delivery system to, as he put it, 'open wide on demand and accept all the fuel that was available'.

So the motor started gobbling gas like it was

dying of thirst, and the result was both immediate and openly terrifying.

A ripping snort erupted from the exhaust pipe and then a high-pitched whining sounded as the motor went insane, and the prop dug into the water like a million shovels all at once.

The boat virtually leaped forward, the bow jerking violently up and then back down, as we started to scream across the water. I had a split second to see that Pooder had managed to hang on, but the skis seemed almost to be airborne like one of those old-time hovercrafts, and I thought that he must have known how to ski expertly after all, when the boat suddenly roared even louder, changed direction, knocking my dad away from the wheel, and began an out-of-control, completely mad, looping curve to the left in the centre of the river.

Again, later – much later – we discovered that the sudden lunging of the propeller when the extra power hit it caused the prop to jam to the side, forcing the boat to careen wildly in a circle.

I felt as if we had climbed onto some bucking-water-bronco amusement-park ride.

My father, who had been literally pitched away from the controls with the sudden sideways slamming motion, was neatly tucked by centrifugal force along the inside of the boat like he was part of the hull. I was holding on with a death grip to the seat with one hand and Carol's collar with the other as we were being whipped up and down like a flag in the wind. But there was plenty of room in the river, and for that half a moment, I thought we had lots of space and enough time to get control of things.

I had forgotten about Pooder.

Who had violently entered the Newtonian realm of physics and was now the living embodiment of the effect of forces on a moving body. While the boat was flying rapidly around in a tight left circle, Pooder, out on the very end of the towrope, was exhibiting the concept of centripetal force, the taut rope pulling inward and preventing Pooder from soaring out over the water with each rotation around the boat.

'At first I thought you were doing it on purpose, you know,' he said when we got the mud cleaned out of his mouth. 'Just to give me a good ride. Then we spun around the second time but everything went faster and faster. The banks of the river were a blur. And by the third or fifth or hundredth time around, I think I approached terminal velocity. I started to have tunnel vision, with a bright light at the end of the tunnel. When I saw my dead grandfather waving at me from the light, beckoning me toward another dimension of existence, that's when I realized it wasn't all for fun, so I decided to let go. I mean, why would he wave? He didn't even like me.'

Long breath, spitting mud, and then: 'I don't remember anything after that.'

'You skipped,' I told him, 'like a flat rock.'

Even though I had been upside down with Carol biting me and Dad kicking me in the gut trying to break free from the force that pinned him to the side of the boat, I still had the wherewithal to watch my best friend skip across the water, the sun still shining on his light hair, his limbs flailing, a fading scream across the water . . .

'You were moving so fast you skipped. I think four times.' I had to fight not to smile, remembering. 'It was hard to count. Everything was moving so fast.'

'I skipped?'

I nodded. 'On the first skip, your trunks and life vest were torn off and you were stone naked the rest of the way.'

He was lying on the shore and tried to raise to look at his body, but his eyes were still packed with mud so he couldn't see much of anything, and he fell back.

'I skipped naked?'

'Totally.' I nodded again. 'You left the skis like an arrow and they beat you to shore. The life jacket was just tatters and we couldn't find your trunks at all. It was incredible. I've never seen anything like it. Not even on film.'

'I'm naked now?'

'Well, not really,' I said in a comforting voice.

'You're more or less caked in mud. On the final skip, you plowed into the muddy riverbank so hard Dad thought you might be buried alive. We had to dig you out when we got ashore.'

'Naked?' He wasn't following well. 'I'm on the shore naked?'

'Dad says it's almost biblical, like you are a new-born babe plucked naked from the river. Don't worry – I've got a swell pair of pink dungarees I can loan you to get home.'

A long silence then, the only sound was Carol trying to lick the mud off Pooder and, far off, some water birds chattering away.

Then Pooder sighed and tried to say something but it came out in almost a whisper:

'What? I couldn't hear you.'

A little louder:

'If it's okay with you guys, I don't believe I want to water-ski anymore today.'

Classic Pooder.

LOSE, WIN, LOSE

After the water-ski incident – which Pooder called Death by Water Ski, hence the name of the previous chapter – things returned to a kind of normal.

As if, Pooder says, anything about this summer could possibly be called normal.

'That water was hard,' he told me days after the skiing adventure as his memory of that afternoon slowly returned. 'I have bruises in places you're never supposed to get bruises. They started out black and blue and then they were purple and now they're turning yellow, and I think there's a good chance I will never have children, which is a shame because I think you will agree that I would make an excellent father.'

We were sitting on a grassy part of the river-bank with Carol, who now regarded the river as an enemy and periodically growled and showed her teeth at the water.

At the moment, she was dozing in the sun and seemed to be trying to run in her sleep while letting out muffled growls and twitching.

'I wonder what she's dreaming about,' I said.

Pooder shrugged. 'Probably a skunk or some small animal that shows fear and is trying to run away. She's a pit bull. They like small things that flee and scurry away in tall grass. It's a call to her more primitive instincts.'

I wondered how he could possibly know that and when did he learn the word *scurry*? And why did he know so much about the predator–prey structure? Pooder was always full of these small – and sometimes not-so-small – surprises.

'Speaking of scurrying things – which means a furtive movement, by the way – how's it going with your dad?' Although Pooder adored my dad as is, he was deeply curious about anything experimental (*see* previous chapter, pages 136–156, for examples).

'I'm back to my regular routine. The squirt bottle seems to be working, which is good. The next thing on the pamphlet is something they call "pleasant confinement", where you keep the subject in a tight area and only let him out to do the whole bathroom business. I don't know how I could pull that off. I mean, there's no way I slap a collar and leash on him without facing the fact that the train has gone off the tracks . . .'

He thought a few moments. 'It's the truck. You could sabotage the truck so it didn't run. That would more or less confine him to home – keep him away from sales or the second-hand clothes shop.'

I shook my head. 'Maybe once in a while, but we need the truck to get feed for the pigs and chickens. And besides, he's too good a mechanic for me to fool him for long.' I sighed. 'I think I'm stuck with the way things are for the time being.'

'And Carol doesn't mind the squirt bottle? The way she did the squirt guns?'

I thought back, reflecting on how the squirt bottle part of the training process had gone, and the first time I had used it as a deterrent.

Which reminded me of the new wrinkle in my ongoing fashion nightmare that would prevent me from becoming lookatable material by the time school started and I was running into Peggy in the hallways.

Shoes.

Somehow, but not surprisingly because the shoe shop and the supermarket both backed out to the same alley and my father never met a dumpster he wasn't willing to dive in, my dad had discovered that the chain shoe shops dumped shoes – threw them away in the rubbish – when they went out of style or demand.

However.

Big however.

In case anyone was observant (and shameless) enough to find this out and make a run for free shoes, thereby skewing the supply and demand chain the shop had going, someone at the shoe shop would ruin the shoes by taking one shoe per pair and running it through a band saw to cut it in half before disposing of them.

'All we have to do,' my dad told me, 'is find a shoe from one pair that isn't cut in half that matches a shoe from another that's not cut in half and, bang, you've got a brand-new pair of matching trainers. Or close to it. Just a little physical effort and no money spent. Might be hundred-dollar trainers, free for the taking. Perfect.'

Oh god, I thought – not swearing, but a prayer for mercy. On top of pink dungarees and tent-size camo T-shirts and boys' small underwear briefs, both of which had been shrunk or stretched to fit a size medium kid, only not really, now I would be expected to wear a pair of trainers that didn't quite match.

Clearly, this was exact right time and place to implement the new squirt-bottle system. I'd start slow and do it at the exact right moment and this time, this technique would work. It had to.

I waited until right before we got to the dumpster. We had started at the supermarket dump for the pig produce haul, stocked up on what we, or rather, the pigs, needed, and that's when I saw SP start to move toward the shoe shop dumpster. I followed closely, scanning the sky. It wasn't overcast or threatening to pour or anything, but there were a few scattered clouds to provide cover for the next step in the training process. I waited, watching, timing it perfectly, and as he reached up for the dumpster lid, I sprayed the back of his neck with my squirt bottle before jamming it in one of the large pockets of my dungarees, which, as my dad had predicted, were very handy and could hold, and hide, almost anything.

'Did you feel that?' he asked, looking at the sky. 'Is that rain?'

I nodded, held out my hand as if feeling for more. 'I think it's going to pour.' I peered up at an almost-pure blue sky. 'We'd better go. We don't want that stuff in the back of the truck to get goobered up by the torrential downpour.'

And, bless me, it worked. Dad nodded and we climbed in the truck and took the pig feed home, and even Carol didn't seem to mind, didn't look at my right eye or show her teeth to me in that scary smile of hers, mostly because she hated rain and always hid in the bathroom when we got bad weather. I had successfully pulled off one of the pamphlet's training methods. Finally.

Or, as Pooder put it, 'You now have another arrow in your quiver. But you have to use it wisely.'

It's usually better to not follow most of Pooder's statements with a question because sometimes you'd get a flood kind of answer. But I was on a high from the success and forgot that discretion is the better part of valour. 'What do you mean?'

'It's common sense. The only way this can work is if SP – that's what you're calling him, right? – doesn't ever know what you're doing. So you have to keep varying your methods, keeping him off guard, so he doesn't get wise to your attempts to alter his behaviour. You've got the squirt bottle and Dairy Queen and diverting his attention with other side issues and maybe doing the broken-truck business now and then that he'll have to take time to fix . . .

see? The trick is you have to keep mixing them up. Maybe throw in a stomach-ache or two from time to time, and the sniffles – can't go shopping if you've got a cold – or, better yet, the runs, because then you don't have to go out in public with him and he'll give you all the privacy you need at home. They all might work, maybe only some will work, but you've got to be crafty about timing and technique, control the frequency and don't repeat them too often, mix it up so SP can't spot the pattern –' He paused to take a breath and I cut in.

'I've been keeping a journal where I write down each reinforcement I get him to perform and each attempt I make to change his incorrect behaviour, so I can keep track of the order of things and not do anything twice,' I pointed out. 'I've already been keeping it pretty random. And I keep my experiment notes hidden out in the feed shed, tucked under the overhang of the roof where it comes down to the wall covered with an old board. I log what I've done when I know he's not looking.'

'Good, I guess.' He frowned. 'Although it's worth

pointing out that, as you may remember, I wasn't sure you should do this in the first place. You have a dad most of us would kill for – but I can see the fashion and social difficulties you might have becoming lookatable if you don't change him.'

Right about then a mud turtle came ashore, saw us, realized its mistake, and hurried back into the water. Carol awakened just in time to see it – Pooder's words – scurry across the mud and under-water, and she took after it. Somehow in all this time living by the river and going on the boat, she still didn't completely understand water and seemed to think she could breathe it. She followed the turtle off the bank and kept going when she hit the water, like a fanged, hair-covered small submarine, totally disappearing under the surface. There was no real body fat on her to make her float – just whip-cord, pit-bull muscle – and she sank like a rock.

She missed the turtle completely and I think she might have drowned if Pooder and I hadn't jumped in and felt around in the muddy water until we felt dog fur and dragged her out.

'Amazing mission focus,' Pooder said. 'Absolutely amazing. She wasn't going to come up for air. Wanted to get it done. Make turtle puree. We could all take a lesson from Carol.'

A side note from Pooder: If your pit bull sinks in muddy water going after a turtle and dips out of sight and needs help to get back to dry land and an oxygen supply, in the interests of personal survival and the preservation of appendages, be careful of what and how you grab. It is significant to note that apparently pit bulls can reach any part of their body with their teeth. End of note. Except to say that Pooder and I took turns helping put plasters on each other because even a warning nip from a pit bull can leave a small puncture wound.

o o o

Summer was fast drawing to an end and the school year was looming, so now began a more serious approach to training the SP. By consistent reference to the journal so as to implement my cautious utilization of the principle of positive reinforcement, alternating with now and then the use of negative reinforcement, I was starting to see an actual difference in Dad's approach to his daily living. I had hopes that I might drag him to a real shop to buy real clothes for me before the first day of school arrived. I had given up on the bike idea and was trying to convince myself that clothes make the man and could help me overcome the terminal uncoolness of arriving at school each day on the bus.

Even Pooder congratulated me on my efforts. 'I think SP has quit pooping on the rug. Metaphorically speaking, of course.' I couldn't believe he used the word *metaphorically* and had to look it up. It means – along with a lot of other meanings – using one description in reference to another. Which is just as well. I can count on the fingers of no hands the number of times my father has ever pooped on a rug.

But Pooder was right. My father *had* changed. I'd been working so hard for so long that I almost missed it when it finally happened.

There came a time when the chicken population cranked up to between twenty and thirty chickens on any given day, and we had eggs coming so fast we couldn't keep a good count of them. Dad put a sign up at the top of the driveway about 'farm-fresh, cage-free, dark-yolk eggs for barter'. But most of the people who showed up just wanted to pay cash and pretty soon we wound up with some sixty dollars in egg money.

That's when I saw him, straight up, with my own eyes, go into an honest-to-goodness shop and buy some fresh socks and brand-new T-shirts and a couple pairs of jeans for me.

And I thought, I have arrived.

At last, I will be marginally lookatable material.

It wasn't much, I'll admit. But it was there, a crack in the foundation of my fashion disaster of a life, a little opening where the light of a better future could come through, and I was happy.

But my dad wasn't.

I mean, it wasn't that he was openly sour or anything, and I thanked him repeatedly for the new clothes – sounding as positive and reinforcing as I could – and he smiled and nodded and said, 'You're welcome.'

But his voice was too soft, almost a whisper, and I could tell that the shopping hadn't pleased him near as much as it delighted and thrilled me. The success of my experiment in correcting his behaviour wasn't as satisfying for him as I thought it should be. The pamphlet had all but guaranteed me that consistent and applied training led to happy owners and equally happy puppies or, in this case, lookatable sons and none-the-wiser SPs.

I let it go, let the off-feeling slide, and took an enormous amount of pleasure in shirts that fit right and socks fresh out of the pack and jeans that didn't say HONEY BUNNY or have as many pockets as a herd of kangaroos.

Things, I thought, would, could, only get better now that I had altered my dad and was ready to head into the new school year and face Peggy as a new man.

Wrong.

Pooder said it was my lack of mission focus. He criticized me taking my success for granted and not paying attention. And I suppose there's something to that – I admit that I got complacent and maybe even a little smug. I mean, there were the socks and T-shirts and jeans that nobody had ever worn before and that fit my body without being washed and shrunk first. Wouldn't you get a little dreamy over something that positive?

The second-to-last weekend of summer, Pooder heard the hang-glider people were back at the same hill again. He wanted to go watch them – he swore that was it, just watch – and so we took our bikes (I was even feeling better about my bespoke – sorry, Pooder made me write that pun – bike these days) and pedalled out to watch the hang gliders who actually did know how to take off at will, glide with full vision, and land without terrorizing a herd of tiny horses.

We arrived early as they were setting up and putting the gliders together and had time to answer Pooder's questions. I noticed that the guys and girls who recognized us kept a barrier of bodies between Pooder and the hang gliders, and across the fields, that the Shetland ponies were crowded along the fence facing the direction of the glider hill, perhaps thinking they might get another shot at destroying the giant predator birds – or whatever they called them in their little horse brains. Once you've successfully changed another living creature's behaviours, you start noticing how people and animals react in case you might need to pull up your training techniques again.

It turned out to be a pleasant afternoon, and Pooder stayed out of trouble mostly because of the ways the glider folks herded him away from the gliders and distracted him with energy bars and sports drinks. Late in the day, we climbed on our bikes and started home and I remember being relaxed and feeling good.

But coming off Murchinson's Hill, you pick up some serious speed, and as the road turns to asphalt and comes into town toward the library, it's a smooth, long, straight, downhill grade, so even if you wanted to slow down (which Pooder never did, of course), it's almost impossible. As we hit town, we were smoking, absolutely smoking, along. I leaned back in my recliner-type recumbent seat and felt the wind whip through my hair and thought

I wouldn't mind if a good downhill grade went all around the world forever and ever.

Until we arrived at the corner of the library where the road took a sharp turn that had been hidden a bit by elm trees and I looked up to see Peggy on her bike just leaving the library.

Directly in front of me.

She would have been in the crosshairs, if I had been looking through a submarine periscope.

Dead centre.

I knew that if I collided with her at this speed I'd kill her and probably myself and the resulting explosion of my bike's light-absorbing black metal and pink-and-moss upholstery would decimate the landscape. I remember thinking, as I was hurtling toward the nightmare of killing or at least seriously injuring myself and the woman I loved: At least I won't die wearing pink dungarees.

So I laid my bike over.

It was the only thing I could do, and to be honest, I didn't do it so much as I couldn't prevent it from happening.

Just took the bike down to my left and skidded for about twenty feet, barely missing the back wheel on Peggy's bike – I think I may have kissed her rear tyre, judging by the busted lip and bloody nose afterward – amidst a great shower of sparks and dust and some words that Pooder said later were 'very short, but quite well stated and descriptive'.

I came to a stop just to the side of Peggy, who had stopped her bike and was standing straddling it, looking down at me, sprawled in a stinging heap of tangled limbs and twisted bike, flashing on the mental image of Pooder's bruises from the water-skiing incident and wondering, briefly, if my set would be more impressive because terra firma is, objectively, much harder to hit at high speeds than good old-fashioned H_2O.

'Are you all right?' she asked.

I was at that moment worrying that I might lose some teeth, had a first-class case of road rash where I had ground the asphalt with my left hip, and was spitting blood. But I managed a short nod and croaked, 'Just fine.'

Which Pooder said was such an obvious lie, he was amazed I didn't burst into flame.

Peggy looked away, bit back a smile, then turned back to me. 'I saw you on television.'

Of course you did, I thought. That makes it perfect. I'm here on my disaster of a bicycle, rendered down to a puddle of gore, and first time we ever speak, you remember me from television, which, prior to this stellar moment was, perhaps, my finest hour of degradation. Of course she saw me on television. How could she not?

'I thought that was so cool.' She looked off again, then back to me, sighed. 'The way you and your dad stay true to your beliefs, living without impacting the environment, is very cool and responsible and kind. We should all be living like you and your father, Carl.' Another pause, then one foot up on the pedal, still standing but ready to go. 'Maybe later we could meet up and you could tell me more about how to make it work. You know, how to live right.'

And, then, with another smile and a quick wave, she pushed the pedal down and was gone. I watched her leave, or started to because my right eye was rapidly swelling shut – apparently my entire face had grazed her rear tyre – but I was numb to any pain even though I was still spitting blood and leaning over so I wouldn't drip it on my new shirt, which had somehow survived my crash landing in pristine condition.

'I never,' Pooder said, 'and I mean never in a thousand years, saw that coming. I mean, out of nowhere, you've found a way to get girls to like you without being lookatable in the least. Who knew that all you had to do was plow your face into the road and bleed a little and, boom, you've got yourself a date. Seriously. Just like that. And she appeared to know your name. What are the odds?'

I floated home on a cloud of bliss. Bloody, still numb from the successful chat with Peggy, and giddy with the promise of better things to come.

But as soon as I entered the trailer, I saw it. Sitting there on the kitchen table.

My father had found my experiment journal.

SUBJECT AND PEER REVIEW EXPERIMENT SUMMARY

The effort I had put into training my dad had seemed to be working over the past few weeks. I mean it wasn't that Dad had started going crazy shopping online or suddenly grubbing for money.

But . . . and it was a huge and hugely appreciated *but*. I had corrected some of his more egregious conduct and I was benefiting from his improved behaviours.

Instead of hunting bargains or barter opportunities, he had started seriously looking at price tags in shops, after voluntarily entering them in the first place, learning how much things did cost in – using his word – ertogs – or Pooder's – coin. He seemed to start to care about new things, previously unused and never discarded things, and how we might get them. He'd even said one afternoon, 'You know, the truck is old and, let's face it, the radio selection is something less than desirable. Maybe we could use it for a down payment on a newer vehicle.'

He'd started watching the want ads in papers and even went on the internet for – I would never have believed it – a job, a real job that paid actual money, and then he applied for, was interviewed, and took a job at a vehicle repair shop out near Oscar's dump. Went to work every morning, came home from work every afternoon, and picked up a pay cheque. Well, it is my dad we're talking about, so the best he could bring himself to do was to work for a man named Wilbur O'Keefe who thought banks were evil and paid in cash and was helping Dad temper his need to rocket-power all fuel injection systems he came across. But he paid in coin, and Dad even admitted that he enjoyed the company and the work, and he kept the money in a jar in the cupboard and spent it without flinching.

And if he wasn't happy – because, even in my

joy, I couldn't help but notice that he didn't seem to be the same as he used to be – I firmly believed I was happy enough for both of us and that, given time, he would come around. Be his old self.

Everything, according to my perspective, was good and getting better and then I crashed and talked to Peggy and I knew I had really done it, really turned things around.

Only then it went bad.

And it was all because of a blasted squirrel. About a month ago a little devil of a red squirrel had showed up and – I didn't believe this either so if you think I'm making it up I don't blame you – started stealing the eggs from our chickens and taking them back to his nest under the work shed. We didn't catch him right away – had no idea what was happening to the eggs – but at last, one evening right before hard darkness, my dad saw him wobble-running, clumsily carrying an egg, and figured out the mystery of the missing eggs: that the squirrel had been stealing eggs at night.

What's amazing is that Carol hadn't got to

him first and put an end to the squirrel and his thieving ways. As thorough as she was with skunk elimination and redistribution, she would, no doubt, have reduced a squirrel to a molecular structure level. A small, scurrying animal in the dark carrying an egg from one of – how she viewed it – her private chickens? She would have vaporized him.

But the squirrel was brainy and crafty and didn't free-range around that garden, but stuck to the safe haven of the feed shed. All the chicken and hog feed in paper sacks sitting there, making a nice balanced diet, in addition to the pilfered eggs, behind a door and walls that Carol couldn't get through, but a skinny little squirrel could.

Carol couldn't get in the shed, but my father could. And did. And surprised the peewadden out of the squirrel. Panic ensued and the squirrel jumped from the chicken-feed sack to an old sawhorse that happened to be close by and from there – pure madness now – to my father's shoulder. That's the part of the story I knew.

The part I didn't know was that the squirrel then did a spring-jump up to the exact place where the roof rafters join the wall, where he landed on the journal's hiding spot, which fell to the ground in front of my father.

Who picked up the little notebook.

And read it.

Damn squirrel.

'I think it's time we had a talk' is what my father said, sitting next to the notebook on the table, when I returned home after a thoroughly excellent day of hang-glider watching and Peggy-talking and smug-isn't-my-life-working-out-grand thinking.

I panicked and told a big lie: 'I don't know what that is.' A burst-into-flame-and-go-straight-to-Hades lie.

'Oh,' he said softly.

I would give a million dollars to not ever hear that 'oh' again. A whisper from inside him, from his soul place.

What have I done? Oh god, oh god, oh god – a prayer. What have I done?

'I thought I could, you know, change how things went around here. Just a little. Just enough so that girls would look at me, well, not all the girls, only one.'

'Peggy.'

'Yes, Peggy.' I must have written about her in the experiment notebook.

'I wasn't going to say anything, but that's not what quality people do, just sweep things under the rug and pretend.'

'When did you find it?'

'Couple weeks ago – the squirrel, you know.'

'Is that why you got a job and traded in the old truck and started buying things?'

'Yeah.' He sounded so sad. 'I hadn't known you felt that way. I always thought you agreed with what we were doing . . . All along I thought you felt the same as me.'

'I did. But then I didn't anymore.'

'Ah, well. At least now we know.'

And he handed me the notebook and turned and left the trailer and didn't say any more.

Pooder was only slightly sympathetic when I ran straight to him for advice. 'You got what you wanted but—'

'But what?'

'But you shifted the paradigm.'

'I did what now?'

'Fundamentally changed everything from the ground up in a sudden and disconcerting way.'

'That was more than I set out to do, to be honest.'

'There's only one thing you can do now.'

'What's that? I'll do anything.'

'You've got to reboot the system. Again. Reboot the reboot.'

'I need more than that to go on.'

'What you've got to do is save what's good from the past and keep what's an improvement in the present and add more quality – your dad will like that, he's all about quality – as you compromise and work together, instead of in opposition to each other, toward a mutually beneficial and acceptable future.'

'And how do I do that?'

'You'll have to figure out the specifics by yourself. He's your dad. But we've got the whole weekend before school starts on Monday to fix everything. More than enough time.' He sounded more confident than I felt as we headed back to the trailer.

Dad was sitting at the table, drinking coffee and petting Carol as he looked out the window. His face was still sad, and my gut tightened for a second. But I took a deep breath and said, 'Who's up for some last-weekend-of-the-summer power-garage-sale bartering and end-of-season dumpster diving for fruit and vegetables?'

He looked up and smiled at me standing in the door.

A quality smile.

A smile of forgiveness and understanding and relief.

Wait.

Just wait until he hears about my ideas for helping Oscar inventory and monetize his junkyard/wealth of supplies, and starting a YouTube channel with videos shot by Pooder for other kids like Peggy interested in his ideas on living life the right way, and speaking to the supermarket about reducing their needless waste by starting a compost pile instead of throwing away perfectly good fertilizer, and working with the shoe shop to donate the shoes instead of destroy them when they go out of style, and maybe even getting CB and Priddy to help start a local farmers' market now that we all have lots of chicken eggs and goat milk, and rewriting that pamphlet – which had some good but not great ideas – that I know we could improve on, given our empirical data and personal experience . . .

Dad and Pooder aren't the only ones who come up with quality ideas.

The End.

Which, of course, is not the end at all . . .

ABOUT THE AUTHOR

Gary Paulsen (1939-2021) wrote more than two hundred books for children and adults. Three of his novels – *Hatchet, Dogsong,* and *The Winter Room* – were Newbery Honor books. In 1997, he received the ALA's Margaret A. Edwards Award for his contribution to young adult literature. His books have sold over 35 million copies around the world.